Fam

Funny short stories about families and family histories

Phil Braverman

Stories in this collection have previously appeared in:

Outsourcing Grandma Sylvia
Return of the Mail Order Bride
Lifeboat Drill
My Aunt Betty's Duck

ISBN: 9781729213049

DEDICATION

Dedicated to everyone who are trying to learn about their family history, and especially those willing to pay a few bucks to have their DNA tested to find out if they're related to God knows who: Atilla the Hun? Donald Trump?

Also by Phil

Outsourcing Grandma Sylvia

Return of the Mail Order Bride

Lifeboat Drill

My Aunt Betty's Duck

ACKNOWLEDGMENTS

For some reason or another, readers requested a book of stories about their ancestors and relatives. As luck would have it, there are many such stories in my previous work. So why bother writing new ones? A big thanks to the "copy" function in MS Word.

CONTENTS

Finding Your Family

Keeping in Touch

Discovering Family History

The Family Business

Happy Occasions

Family Secrets

FINDING YOUR FAMILY

Cousins

Amaze yourself

Uncover your ethnic origins and find new relatives with our simple DNA test.

Only $59

Genealogy has become a very popular science. Many people subscribe to one of several Internet-based services that help you trace your ancestry and help you find relatives in the old country. But, perhaps there are people in the old country looking for their relatives in America? Looking for you!

Phone rings….

Hello. Who is this?

Hello, back! This is your cousin, Mendel.

Mendel who?

Mendel Shumpski, Mendel Shumpski from Grodno, Poland.

I don't know anybody in Poland, you must have the wrong number.

But we're cousins…

How do you know we're cousins?

I used the web site *Findfolks.com* and clicked on — *Find Wealthy Cousins*—we're related on your mother's side…maybe your father's side too. Grodno, it's a small town…

How did you get my number?

Findfolks.com sells the numbers for an extra 15 bobkies.

Listen, I don't have any cousins in Grodno, they were all wiped out during the war.

Well, we weren't. How could I be calling if I

was wiped out?

How do I know this isn't some kind of scam?

Would I scam my own cousin?

I guess not. So you say we're cousins, so what? I have a lot of cousins.

If they are your cousins they are my cousins too! We want to meet them.

Who's We?

My wife Rebka, my six sons and three daughters. We're going to be on vacation in West Palm Beach where you are. It seems like a beautiful spot to visit and see the family.

What family?

Your family, my family. Get it?

I still don't believe we're related. How did you find me again? Listen, I have caller ID. You're not calling from the old country, it looks like you're calling from somewhere very close.

That's right, we are at the bus station waiting

for the goat to be unloaded.

What goat?

Schmuel, the family pet.

I don't think most hotels will take a goat.

That's what I was calling about; we need a place to stay. We hear that in America you all have big houses and yards so it should work out just fine.

Well, we don't, we're retired and live in a mobile home park, no overnight visitors, no pets.

You mean you're not rich?

No, we're not rich.

My cousin Reuven Sheveski in America is rich, the *FindFolks* web site said so. So, who am I speaking to?

Harry O'Brien. As in Harry and Ruth O'Brien.

You're' not Reuven Sheveski?   Reuven and Sylvia?

No.

Well, I guess I must have the wrong number—(*shouts*) Rebka, don't unload the goat!

Well, I'm sorry...

That's all right. We'll stay at the Marriott, I have   points. We'll sneak the goat in too.

And, you came all this way from your shtetl?

What shtetl? We have a villa in Vilnius with a pool. I'd hoped to connect and fly you both over there, we're on a lake, it's very beautiful...

Well, I guess we won't see it. I hope you find your family soon. Goodbye, Mendel.

Goodbye, Harry.

hangs up

Reuven, who was that on the phone?

Nobody, Sylvia. Wrong number.

Lunch at Costco

We were sitting in the Costco snack bar having foot long dogs, my teenage daughters and I. Morwenna had a hotdog and Petula had a Polish. Suddenly a big blackbird flew very near us and landed on the shopping cart of a very surprised lady shopper. He cocked his head at me and his gaze seemed very familiar. The lady moved her cart and he flew off only to return seconds later, this time landing on the floor next to me. My curiosity grew as he looked me straight in the eye. I threw him a piece of my hot dog bun and he hopped around with it in his beak for a minute or two before swallowing. Then he fluttered down and landed near my feet.

"Do you believe in reincarnation?" I asked the girls.

"I don't know, depends." said Morwenna.

"Girls, that bird reminds me of someone very familiar. I think it might be my father." They both giggled at the thought. But just then the blackbird hopped up on the edge of the table where I was sitting. I don't know why, but I began to talk to it.

"Dad...is that you?"   The girls burst out laughing, and after a couple of more bites of their lunch, went off to shop, leaving me alone with the blackbird. "Dad?" I asked again.

"Yes it's me, Son," he answered in a squeaky bird-like voice, "I knew someday I'd run into you again. How the heck are you?"

"I'm fine, Dad, but whatever are you doing being a blackbird? You've been dead a long time, you know. Have you always been a blackbird?"

"No, Son. First I came back as a cat but that didn't last too long. You see I choked on a fish bone. Should have been more careful, but hell, what do you expect of a cat?   Then I came back as a goldfish, and you know they don't last long. Boy was I dumb as a lamp post!   I over-ate, bellied-up and got flushed down the toilet by Willy, my 8 year-old owner."

"Next, I came back as a squirrel. It was really a lot of fun being a squirrel, but kinda cold at night in the park. Then one day while crossing the road

I couldn't make up my mind which way to run...cross or no cross? While I was thinking it out, a Prius got me (2012, I think). Now I'm a red-winged blackbird and having more fun than in any of those other lives, believe you me! I'm smart. I can fly. I get lots of good things to eat, I have a nice nest in a good neighborhood and I've got a great wife, Leslie. How many people...er...birds can say that?"

"Gee, Dad, that's wonderful. But what on earth are you doing in Costco?"

"Actually, Son, I work here. I'm in security, on the Loss Prevention Team. I fly around and watch the shoppers. Although it's hard to stuff a set of tires under your coat, you'd be surprised what they can steal. I have a little microphone right here under my wing, and if I spot a shoplifter I call it in and circle till help arrives. Did you know I was Employee of the Month in April!"

"My gosh. are you the only bird working here?"

"No, there are two of us: me and Leslie. She's my wife. She's really nice and I'd like you to meet her. She's going on her break soon and flying here to meet me for some hotdog bun scraps--like you fed me. And by the way, thank you for that, you were always a good son. You'll really like Leslie. When she was a human, she taught piano. She's very musical. You ought to hear her chirp some Brahms."

"Dad, quite frankly I'm having a hard time with all of this."

"I know, Son, it's a lot to swallow if you'll forgive the pun. Here comes Leslie, now. Hi, honey-bird!"

"Hi, Ralph. Sorry I'm a bit late. We had a spill on aisle 7 and I had to call it in. It turns out it was something yummy, so I stayed around to have a taste while they were cleaning up."

"I hope you didn't spoil your lunch, you know you always eat like a...well, never mind. I've saved you a few choice bits that I put away up in our rafter. We can go to lunch in just a few minutes--you have plenty of time left on your break. But first there is someone I want you to meet. Leslie, this is my son, Eric."

"Hello, Eric, I've heard nothing but good things about you."

"Hello Leslie, it's a real surprise and a pleasure to

meet you, too. Speaking of meeting someone, Dad, Leslie, I want you to meet your granddaughters, Morwenna and Petula. Here they come now."

"Wow, Son, what beautiful girls! Hello, girls, I'm your Grandpa, Ralph. It's a pleasure to meet you both. And this your Step-Grandma, Leslie."

"Hi, girls, I also had two daughters in my human life," said Leslie. "One became a lumberjack and the other works on a commercial fishing trawler. I see the lumberjack from time to time but it's just too much for me to fly way out to that trawler at my age."

"Daddy," asked Morwenna, "are those birds actually talking to us?"

"Yep really! It's hard to believe isn't it? But I told you before you left, I thought the bigger bird was my dad. And he is...well, was."

"OMG," they said in unison. "Talking birds, and we may be related to them?"

"Well, I certainly am, that's my dad with the piece of cheese in his beak."

"Listen Son," interrupted Ralph. "I really need to

eat and get back to work; Leslie too. I'll look for you next time you come into the store. Gonna give you the birds-eye tour (wink). Gotta fly now."

"Bye, Grandpa, bye, Leslie." The girls waved to the birds as they flew off. "Hope we see you again. Daddy, can we go home now?"

Alex and Alec

I'll never forget walking into that Under-40 Professional Singles event and seeing myself in the mirror. Except it wasn't a mirror, it was another person, another me. My doppelganger, I think is the expression for it.

My named is Alex. Alex Rifkn. I'm a professional musician. I play piano for the New York Philharmonic. It's a great job if you like music. But if you want to know the truth, I always wanted to play professional baseball. Anyway, I walked up to this look-a-like guy and introduced myself.

"Hi, I'm Alex Rifkn. I can't help noticing you look just like me, or I look just like you, whatever."

"Son of a gun," he said. "You do. Er, I do. What are the odds? Listen, you're not going to believe this, my name is Alec, too."

"You're kidding me," I said. "Don't tell me

your last name is Rifkn."

"I won't because it's not. It's Axlrod. Alec Axlrod. C'mon, Alex, let me buy you a drink. The single ladies here can wait."

"So Alex," he said to me, "what do you do for a living?"

"I play the piano, concert piano," I told him. "How about you?"

"I'm a professional baseball player," he said, "a late inning relief pitcher for the Mets."

"Wow, I'm a big baseball fan," I said. "How come I don't know you?"

"I just came up from the minor leagues a couple of months ago," he said. "I'm new to town. That's why I'm here at this singles event." "So, Alex," he said. "How did you get to be a professional piano player?"

"Well," I told him, "my mother was a musician, my father, too. She made me practice from the time I was a little kid. Day in, day out. All I ever wanted to do was play professional baseball but she wouldn't let me. I had to sneak out late in the day and throw a few pitches."

"Isn't that something," he said. "I wanted to be a professional piano player, but my mom insisted I play baseball. She played women's baseball in college and was a big star. I had to sneak and practice my piano late in the day when she wasn't around. Pretty hard to play piano when you've been throwing pitches for the last four hours. Especially knuckle balls."

"My turn Alec," I said to him. "so, tell me how you became a professional baseball player?"

"Same way you got your job; practice, practice, practice. I played college ball, and tried out for the minor leagues, you know, *A minor* (forgive the pun). Listen, let's get together sometime soon. I'd like to show you what I can do on the piano. I'm really pretty good."

"And I pitch for an adult league. We're only

amateurs but our game is terrific."

***

Alec and I became good friends. We played duets on the piano. Alec is quite accomplished, and he caught pitches from me, and could not believe the speed of my fastball. We began to see a lot of one another. We double dated and when he was not on road trips with his team, we attended a lot of concerts. One day, Alec came up to me with an idea.

"Listen Alex, he said. "why don't we swap jobs once in awhile? I know you can really pitch, and you know I am great piano player. We could both realize our dreams, don't you think."

"Wow," I said. Isn't that a little risky? We could lose our jobs."

"Not a chance," he said. "I'll coach you and you can coach me until we get it right. I won't be nervous, I play in front of more people than you ever will."

"Lets give it a shot, 'I said, "It's the chance of a lifetime for me to pitch in a Mets game, oh, wow."

***

So Alec and I began rehearsing. I was scheduled to perform Brahms No. 3 Piano Concerto in a few months.

We worked on that. I taught him my technique and he was able to pick up the nuances of the piece rapidly. Smart guy, that Alec, and very talented. He prepared me for a Mets/Giants game. He had all the stats on the Giant hitters and what kind of pitches I should throw in late innings. We worked on my curveball and slider.

The big days arrived and my concert piece was first on the program. Alec looked great in my tux, a perfect fit. He wasn't nervous at all and neither was I.

The performance went off with out a hitch. The audience loved it. They applauded and laughed when Alec waved a Mets cap at them that he'd brought along, and fist-bumped the orchestra conductor. The reviews in the paper next day were wonderful. *Such energy and athleticism on the keyboard*, one music critic said.

For my part, I was sent into a Mets game in the 7th inning to retire the Giants in the 7th 8th and 9th. I was really on that day, recording five strikeouts, three pop flies and a groundball, that I fielded for the final out. Alec was in the stands, of course, and ribbed me no end for taking a bow, shaking the umpires hand and asking our team in the dugout to come out and take a round of applause. What a day that was! The sportswriters commented on my rhythmic windup and delivery.

We did this several times over the rest of the concert and baseball season. What a thrill.

One late afternoon, over beers, Alec and I got to talking. He said, "Alex, you know our interests and talents are so similar, do you think we really could be twins?"

"Impossible," he said, "we may look alike but I wasn't adopted. Were you?"

"Not that I know of, but maybe we need to ask, or get a blood test or something."

"Let's just ask our folks outright. I'm going to call my mom and flat out ask if I was adopted."

"I'll do the same," said Alec.

And we did just that.

I am my Brother's Catcher

Do I have a brother? Could Alec Axlrod and I really be twins? What an exciting thought, to be closely related to a major league pitcher.

"Hi, Mom," I said, over the phone. "This is kind of an awkward question, maybe even a stupid question, but was I by any chance adopted?"

"Yes, you were honey, we didn't want to upset you, we didn't think it was that important. Why are you asking now, after all these years?"

"Good grief Mom! I met this guy in the City, and he and I are so alike it's spooky."

"Well, that's because you were a twin. But there was only one of you left by the time we got to the adoption agency."

"Holy crap, Mom. Do you have any information about our birth-parents?"

"Sure, honey, we exchange cards every Holiday season. No problem. Just a minute, I'll give you their address."

I called Alec and reported this amazing conversation, and he said,

"You know what Alex, the same damn thing just happened to me. I said, "Mom, was I adopted? Am I a twin?" She said, "Of course you are, but we only got you. You were the cutest little thing when we brought you home—big hands though. I just knew you'd turn out to be a great ballplayer like dad and myself."

"Then I asked her if she knew how to get I touch with my birth parents."

"Sure, she said. "Your father and I see them all the time, they're in our bridge club. The Mishkines. They're kinda boring people, but they're nice enough."

"Alec this is crazy," I said to him on the phone. "So we are twins, Are you up to paying our birth parents a visit?"

"Sure Bro. Let's do it."

And we did. The address we were given was in a nice neighborhood on Long Island, near where Alec grew up and played little league baseball. We rang the bell and a nice looking middle-aged lady answered.

"Are you Mrs. Rose Mishkine?" I asked her.

"Yes, yes, I am. Who wants to know?"

"Well, I'm Alex Rifkn and this is Alec Axlrod. I think we're your twin sons."

"Yes, well of course you are. Won't you come in boys, I have some nice coconut cake."

"Wow," I said, between bites. "It must have been hard for you to give us up. Were you an unmarried couple at the time? We're you in financial trouble? Giving us up must have been a very difficult thing to do."

"No, actually it was pretty easy. Your father and I were married and had good jobs, but we just never wanted kids. Much too noisy. You two were an accident. We didn't want you, so we gave you up for adoption. It's a lot easier to get rid of singles so we split you up. Sorry about that. Please don't take it personally. It looks like you did find each other and that's nice."

"Oh, my goodness," said Alec, rolling his eyes. "Tell us about yourselves, were you musical, did you like sports?"

"No, no, nothing like that. Your father works in accounting, and I'm a school librarian. We're not musical, although we do have a record player. Mostly we like it quiet when we're home. And neither of us watch sports. Your father thinks it's a waste of time. What do you boys do for a living?"

"Alec is a major league relief pitcher for the New York Mets, and I'm a pianist with the New York Philharmonic."

"That's nice," she said, "Although we kind of hoped you'd grow up to be pharmacists or dentists, or vets. I guess you can't have everything, can you? But it sounds like both of you have good jobs and health insurance. That's nice. Listen, I have to go to the store now. But stop by anytime you're in the area. Well, maybe you better call first, we're kind of busy.

We said goodbye and left. We drove away and neither of us spoke a word in the car for about ten minutes. Finally Alec said, "You know what, let's go throw some pitches and then grab some beers and listen to Mozart."

"Fine, you know there's a Jewish Singles Twins Club cocktail party Saturday night?

"Great, I'm up for it," said Alec.

***

Later that day:

"Jack," said Rose Mishkine to her husband, you'll never guess who stopped by today!"

Phil Braverman

Everyone, Meet Lloyd!

"I've had it," said Miriam Greenbelt woefully. "I'm getting too old for this. Henry, can you get this TV program to record on our machine? I just can't seem to do it."

"What? You mean we can record? Did I know that?"

"Of course, dummy. I've been recording Downton Abbey for years now, it comes on after we go to bed. I just forgot how to do it."

"Call your son Lenny. Maybe he can come over and record it for us."

"Don't be foolish Henry, you know Lenny moved to New York six months ago."

"He did? Why didn't anybody tell me? What are we going to do for help around here?"

"I don't know, Henry. It's gonna be a real problem. Maybe we need to get some help in the house."

"What kind of help? You mean like a handyman

or a maid? Is that expensive?"

"Don't worry, Henry, I'll look into it. Maybe someone in my Mahjong club has an idea."

The very next morning...

"Miriam, look at this story in the newspaper. It's about robots that can do all kinds of things for you. The company who makes them is called *Helpful Housebots*. Maybe we should look into a robot to record your TV programs and do other stuff around the house."

"That is the most absurd thing I've ever heard of! Are they expensive?"

"Well, it says in the article there's a company who will lease you one for about half the cost of a live-in maid. They give their number here. I'm going to write it down."

***

Another week passed, and this time both Miriam and Henry forgot to put out the garbage. They were stuck with a full smelly can for a whole week.

"Again with a problem, Henry. Can't you make

a note to yourself?""

"I did Miriam, I did make a note. I just can't find it. Listen, I still have the number of the company who makes those household help robots. I'm going to call them up right after my nap."

Henry contacted *Helpful Housebots* and after discussion with the sales person, ordered a robot on a ten day trial. On delivery day the Housebot, named "Lloyd" the technician told them, was installed and plugged in to charge its batteries.

***

The next morning, Henry and Miriam woke up to the smell of pancakes and freshly brewed coffee. Cautiously, they dressed and went down to the kitchen.

"Oh, good morning, folks, I'm Lloyd, your Housebot. I hope you like pancakes. Would you like me to call you Mr. and Mrs. Greenbelt, or can I use your first names? I was programmed to know it's Miriam and Henry, right?"

"Well, we hardly know you," said Miriam, "but I guess since you're going to live with us we should be on a first name basis. By the way, did you unplug yourself? You don't need us to wind you up or anything?"

"No problemo, Miriam. I can do just about anything. Matter of fact, I woke up...'er charged up early, and I've been doing little things around the house, I hope you don't mind."

"What little things—you didn't break anything did you Lloyd?"

"Au contraire, Miriam. I changed two light bulbs way up in the ceiling. Then I waxed the floor in the dining room, I emptied the dishwasher and scrubbed the pots I found in the sink, and I cleaned the oven. Then I brought in the paper and noticed your screen door lock wasn't working and I fixed that too. When I was getting the paper, I saw a couple of nasty grease spots on your driveway and I cleaned those up, and then I got rid of some dog poop on your lawn. I would have vacuumed the house but I didn't want to wake you with the noise."

"Pinch me, Henry!" said Miriam

"Why should I pinch you?"

"Never mind. Listen Lloyd, can you deal with the TV remote and do recordings of my programs?"

"Piece of cake, Miriam. Just tell me what you want recorded. I'm real good with electronics, being electronic myself and all. I can even call the cable company to report a problem. Listen, if you need help with your computer I'm pretty expert in all the email and word processing systems. I can download stuff for you and show you how to use Facebook and YouTube and just about anything,"

"YouTube, schmootube, just turning the computer on and off would be a big help," said Miriam,

"I can drive, too," said Lloyd. "I'll bet you'd like someone to drive you places, especially at night, right? I have a license but we'll need to call your insurance man to cover me. I can do that for you, too. I've already memorized both your voice patterns. In fact, I can make calls for you or take incoming calls and deal with those telemarketing jerks.

"And speaking of calls," said Lloyd. "Do you mind if I use your phone? I need to call my brother Maurice, who got placed last week on the other side of town."

"Don't be silly, Lloyd, of course we don't mind. After all that work you've just done, you are fantastic!" said Miriam.

"Oh, hi, Maurice, Lloyd here at the Greenbelts. Just checking in to see how you're doing at the Sitzmark house."

"It's pretty nice here, Lloyd. Ben and Sylvia are treating me like a king. Of course I've been working more like a serf than a king, but you know how that is… that's what we're here for, right? The weather's been great so I've been working in their yard. I stained their deck, weeded the flower patch, and mowed the lawns. They have a pool and I said to them, hey, I can take care of your pool for you, test the chemicals, change the filter, vacuum the bottom, and put the cover on and off. It would be my pleasure. And the other day, I drove their grandkids to their ice skating lessons. This morning I've been writing thank you notes for the Stizmarks—it was their 40th anniversary and they got a lot of cards and gifts. I catered their party Saturday night and we all had a great time. How about you, Lloyd?"

As the months passed, Henry and Miriam grew greatly dependent on Lloyd, and they had become quite fond of him as well. He became more and more a member of their family. He now did all the shopping, cooking, and washing up. He made fantastic matzo ball soup, and at Passover, led their Seder, and he read the parts in Hebrew, beautifully. Miriam and Henry decided to formally adopt him.

"Lloyd," said Miriam, "you've been with us six months now and it seems there is just nothing you can't do. I have to tell you how much we appreciate having you around, you really are part of our family and Henry and I would like to adopt you as our son."

"Oh, my, Miriam! That would be fantastic, but you already have a son. What about Lenny?"

"Lenny, schmenny. Look, that schmendrick, he never calls, and now that he's moved to New York, we hardly ever see him. You're here for us. You're our son now. What do you say?"

So Lloyd, who never had parents, agreed, with pleasure. The Greenbelts cleared it with *Helpful Housebots*. They bought out his lease, and signed a long-term maintenance agreement. Then they filled out formal adoption papers. The Child

Protective Services people were brought in to advise on this unusual event, but they threw up their hands and said, *"It's crazy but what the hell, let'm adopt the Android. What do we care."*

"Let's do something to celebrate our adopted son," said Miriam. "A bris is out, but how about a big party, and we'll invite all our friends."

"Great idea, Miriam. Maybe Lloyd can get his brother Maurice to cater?"

That Saturday Night...

"Everyone, meet our new son Lloyd!" said Miriam proudly.

Lloyd was simply charming, and had the guests laughing all evening with his stories and jokes. Henry and Miriam were just beaming with delight and pride. And of course, Lloyd and his brother Maurice did all the cleaning up. Who could ask for a better son?

Lloyd became even more attentive and useful. He made sure they took their meds at night and kept their doctors appointments. He stood in line for stamps at the post office, wrote checks, paid bills, and changed Henry's hearing aid batteries.

He painted their kitchen, visited sick friends for them, cleaned the barbeque, sprayed the fruit trees, did their gift shopping, cleaned out Henry's garage, and so much more.

Growing fonder of Lloyd every day, Miriam and Henry changed their will. They left some cash to Lenny, but left the bulk of their estate, including the house, to their new son, Lloyd. Lloyd called Maurice to tell him the good news.

"That's wonderful Lloyd," said Maurice. *"Ben and Sylvia really like me too but I don't know if they are ready to adopt. Time will tell."*

"Listen, Maurice, Saturday is Shabbos, my day off, why don't we get together. I'll ask my mom if I can use the car and we'll go to Best Buy Electronics and try to pick up some girls."

"Sounds great, Lloyd. Swing by and pick me up at 11:30. We'll do lunch."

Staying in Touch

Barry

After the funeral, my sister, Melanie and I walked in silence around the streets of our hometown. Our mom and dad, Myra and Morris, had passed, just hours from each other. The same age, they had been joined at the hip for almost 70 years, so we didn't have much to complain about.

We wandered around the old section of town and poked our heads into an antique shop that had some interesting looking stuff in the window. While rummaging in the back of the store, I spotted an old kerosene lamp, the kind used before the houses in our town were wired for electricity. I remembered seeing a lamp like this at my grandma's house. I decided to buy it as a remembrance of the town we grew up in.

In the kitchen, back at my folks' house, I started to clean the lamp a bit. I wiped the dust off the glass bowl and shined up the brass body. And, what the hell, as I was rubbing the brass with a cloth, *poof*, a ghost-like person appeared, rising out of the top of the glass dome.

"Excuse me," I said. "Who are you? What are you? You scared the crap out of me."

"My name is Barry, Barry Kritzer. Sorry, Master, I didn't mean to jump out so fast. It's just that I've been in that damn lamp so long. I've got to tell you, it's really cramped in there."

"Melanie," I bellowed. "C'mere. You won't believe this!"

"Holy Smokes, Mike," said Melanie. "Who is this guy, and what's he doing in our kitchen?"

"He says his name is Barry. He popped right out of the lamp I bought at the antique store."

"Listen, folks," said Barry, "relax, I won't bother you. I'd just like 24 hours out of that lamp and then I'll go back. Promise. And if you let me stay, I'll grant you one wish. What would you like? Something for the house? Just about anything within reason, is on me. By the way, I'm sorry about your mom and dad."

"How do you know about them?"

"Well..."

"You know, Michael," said Melanie, "I wish we could spend a few minutes with mom and dad so we could ask them some questions we should have asked years ago, about how their parents got to this town from the old country, what they did for a living, stuff like that."

"Yeah, that would really be great, Melanie. I wish we could talk to them one more time."

"Well, that's a good wish," said Barry. "That's something I can do. I can let you visit with them, but only for half an hour. Let's do it right now. Are you ready?"

"Oh, wow, I guess we are."

"Ok, kids, here we go!"

another poof of something...

Michael: *Ma, Pa, we can see you!*

Myra: *Oh, hello, Michael, hello Melanie. Look, Morris it's the kids. What's this all about? How was the funeral?*

Morris: *You busted up our bridge game!*

Melanie: *Ma, Pa, Michael bought a lamp, and it turned out to be a magic lamp.. And, there is a Genie, and we got to have one wish.*

Michael: *Yes, and we both…*

Myra: *You bought a lamp, how much did you pay for it?*

Morris: *I bet they paid too much. You should have gone to my friend Max. He would have given you a good deal on the lamp.*

Myra: *Don't listen to him, Max sells only junk.*

Morris: *There's a good living in junk, Myra.*

Melanie: *Ma, you don't understand, we got this lamp, and we both wished we could have a chance to talk to you one more time and ask you some family…*

Morris: *Wait a minute. You bought a lamp just so you could talk to us? Get that, Myra, crazy kids!*

Myra: *That's the dumbest thing I've ever heard. You children should be more careful with your money.*

Michael: *But Mom, Dad, listen. We got a wish and, the Genie, his name is Barry...*

Morris: *A Genie named Barry. That's meshugana. There's no such thing, is there, Myra?*

Myra: *Yes, there is, Morris, you had a cousin Jean, we used to call her Jeannie. Is that who you two talked to? Cause if it is she was no good, and I wouldn't believe her for a minute. She ran off with a wholesale corned beef salesman and left her husband George...*

Morris: *No, Myra, not George, it was Gordon, she left Gordon.*

Myra: *I think it was George, Morris.*

Barry: *It <u>was</u> Gordon, Myra.*

Melanie: *Barry, don't butt in. Mom, Dad! Please stop for a minute. We want to ask you some questions about the family.*

Myra: *Whose family, mine or your father's? Your father had some pretty shady characters on his side.*

Morris: *Listen who's talking! Chicken ranchers; I*

married into.

Michael: *Ma, Barry gave us only half an hour and the time is almost up.*

Myra: *Then maybe you can get your money back for the lamp?*

Morris: *I'll bet that guy on the street is not in business anymore.*

Michael: *We didn't buy it from a guy on the street, we bought it from an antique store and Barry came with it. He's trying to help us.*

Morris: *My Uncle, Yonkel, used to have an antique store, didn't he, Myra?*

Myra: *It was more like a junk shop.*

Barry: *I remember your Uncle Yonkel!*

Morris: *You know, there's a lot of money in junk, always has been.*

Myra: *You already said that, Morris.*

Morris: *I did?*

Barry: *You did, Morris.*

Morris: *So sue me!*

Myra: *Is that the kind of questions you have kids? Do you want to know about Uncle Yonkel?*

Barry: *Better hurry up!*

Melanie: *No, Ma, we want to know about your family, and Pa's, and how they got here from the old country.*

Myra: *Well, it's a long story. Maybe you ought to buy another lamp?*

Barry: *Sorry, kids. Sorry, Morris and Myra. Time's up.*

Morris: *Bye, kids. Bye, Barry.*

The Very Social Medium -- Part 1

My mom's business was down lately, she complained to me recently. She's a medium, a paranormal professional, and believe you me, she really has psychic powers. She has her own practice: *The Spirits Shoppe.* As I was growing up she knew everything I did, which made it kind of tough, especially when I discovered girls. But that was a long time ago. I'm in my 30's now and have my own software business. I could easily send mom money, but she'll have none of that. She enjoys her work and just wishes her business were better.

But let me explain what she does. Basically, as I understand it, she is able to connect her clients to their dearly departed friends or relatives. She does this at a séance session, and when she goes into some kind of trance she is able to connect with a departed spirit. No, really, I've been to some of her sessions and it works. Sometimes the voice of the departed comes out of her lips. I've got to tell you, that is really spooky. You should see the look on her client's faces the first time it happens! Sometimes the spirit is asked a question and you just hear rapping on the table; two for yes, one rap for no. You're probably familiar with that situation. Or she might use a Ouija board where mom's hands and the client's hands guide the spirit's message which is then spelled out one letter at a time. Boy, is that ever slow.

So mom and I are having lunch today and I have a hunch she's going to ask me for some help, which I'll be glad to do. By the way, her name is Madam Rose, Rose Lieberman, MP (Masters in Parapsychology). My name is Al, I'm a computer geek. Come join us for lunch.

"Hi Ally, thanks for taking me to lunch."

"Good to see you Mom. You look well."

"I am well, but as I told you over the

phone Ally, my business stinks lately. Oh, plenty of people are dying every day, that's not the problem. The problem is that my newer clients want instant gratification, they don't want to sit through a long boring séance. They want a speed dial connection to the departed. How am I going to do that? A good séance takes patience and I have to be all psyched up myself, in order to pull it off. It's a slow process. And then there's marketing. Used to be that word-of-mouth was my main source of clients, but many of my older clients who referred me are dropping off. What am I supposed to do, make cold telemarketing calls from the obituary pages?"

"The obits, not a bad idea. Mom," I said. "But telemarketing is kind of old hat these days. You need to computerize your business. Everyone is doing it. You've got to use Social Media, like Facebook, for example. Maybe even create your own website. I could build it for you. If you could communicate with the departed by messaging, what a great thing that would be. In fact you could call it the *Grateful Dead.com.*"

"I'd be willing to try anything, if you think it might work. Lets do it, Ally. We'll figure out a name later."

So Al built his mother a social media website where she could be "friends" with people, er, spirits on the other side. What Rose would have to do, he told her, is contact the departed, and tell them how to sign on as members. "No easy job," he said.

'"You know what, Ally, I think I'll get in touch with your father. He was always good with computers when he was alive, and he sure could waste a lot of time on Facebook and LinkedIn and those other sites. I think he could set all this up for the departed loved ones of my clients."

"Great idea Mom. How about naming the service, *Everafter.com*?"

"Let me talk to your father first. We can pick a name later."

So Rose, after a nice class of wine, put herself in a Class 2 trance and contacted her late husband, Sol.

"Oh hello, Rose dear. How are you? How's Al doing?"

"We're all fine here. Ally is doing well, although he's still not married. How are you doing up there, Sol?"

"Good, I guess if you can call being made out of Ectoplasm good. But then again, as I've told you, that's the stuff that lets me use my computer keyboard, and lets me lift the tables and do the knocking during your séance's. Right, Rose? Listen, what made you summon me? It's not our anniversary is it? Did I forget again?"

"No, Solly, it's not our anniversary. Ally gave me a great idea to pump up my business—by having me connect the departed with their living loved ones by computer. Instead of you lifting tables and rapping yes, and no, and me speaking for them, we'd hook the client and the departed up to a web site and they could Instant Message, or Like, or Follow, or whatever it is people do to communicate these days.

"How in heck is that going to work, Rose?"

"I'm the one who will make the connection Solly, as I always have, and clients would still have to come to my studio for now, but Al is working on a mobile version: *Comeback.com* he calls it, or whatever. Listen, we have time to choose a name later. What I need you to do Solly, is make contact with my client's dearly departed and teach them how to sign up and sign on. It's free to them, and it always will be. I'll collect the cash on this end."

"Well, it sounds like it might work. What's in it for me Rose? I'm pretty busy up here, and you know Halloween is only a couple of weeks away. Say, maybe we could call it, *That'sthespirit.com*, I like that."

"Well you'd be helping me a lot, Solly.

You know you didn't leave me much, having to schlep to work every day, and at my age too. Besides some of my clients are wealthy widowers. Maybe you can make friends with some of their good-looking departed wives. I wouldn't mind."

"Over my dead body, Rose! You were always my sunshine, my only sunshine. And you know I didn't make much as a bartender on an oil rig. Okay, I'll do it. Maybe we could call it *Missme.com,*or how about *Whine&Sprits.com?*

"Later with the names, Solly."

Al finished the new website. And, with Sol's help, they ran some tests with a couple of Rose's late Mah Jongg partners, and with Irving, a late fishing buddy of Sols. The web site worked fine although, the profile pictures of the departed were really awful; sometimes white or grey luminous, waxy, hazy figures. Sol explained this was due to the Ectoplasm, that, even when perfect, images appear soft and vaporous. "Oh, well, thought Rose, I'll have my living clients send me their favorite pictures and we can upload them to the web site. Ally tells me we can do that."

And with great fanfare, new incarnation of her *SpiritsShoppe* was launched with the final name of *HoneyI'mHome.com*™ She and Al and Sol could hardly wait till the first client tried it. One of her clients and a good friend, Doris Pincus, was scheduled to come in the day after tomorrow.

The Very Social Medium – Part 2

Madam Rose's first customer at her new Psychic practice, *HoneyI'mHome.com* was her long-time friend Doris Pincus. Doris had lost her husband Harry two years ago, and had been Rose's client ever since. Contacting Harry had never been easy. Rose told her about the new web site and convinced her that she really ought to try this new way of contacting him.

"How does it work Rose?

"Well, Doris, I go into a trance, as I always do. In order to summon the spirits I have to tune myself to the vibrations of your husband Harry, in the spirit world. When I've made contact and I give the signal, you log in to *HoneyI'mHome.com* It's a website my son, Al, made for me. Then, when you see me with a glassy-eyed look you type in Harry's name and the program will ask if you want to be *spirit* *"friends"* with him. You click *yes.* I've already messaged my late husband Sol to help Harry on his end. He'll help him connect and then you two can talk, er, message. Don't forget to wake me up when you're done."

"Okay, here goes my trance, type in your messages, Doris."

Typing a message>

Hello, Hello. Harry dear, is that you? Can you hear me?

Typing a message>

Yes, Doris, I can see your message. What do you want? Did I leave the stove on or something?

Typing a message>

No, Harry, the stove is fine. How are you sweetheart? Are you eating properly?

Typing a message>

Yes, yes, I'm eating. Is that why you called me up from the beyond?

Typing a message>

You went so suddenly Harry, was there something you wanted to tell me?

Typing a message>

I don't think so, Doris, although I may have forgotten to mention that Doctor Brodsky told me not ever to eat Gribenes, and I think that was the last thing you fed me.

Typing a message>

Oh, my, Harry dear. I knew it was all my fault. I knew I killed you. I'm so sorry!

Typing a message>

Not your fault, Doris. I loved Gribenes, still do. Listen Doris, I got to run now. Nice talking to you. Give the grandkids a hug for me.

Typing a message>

Oh, Harry, I miss you. I'll be back in touch next week.

Typing a message>

Fine, Doris, but don't message me on Wednesdays, that's my pinochle day. Say, I hope this call isn't costing you an arm and a leg. It's free on my side. Sol Lieberman set this up for me, do you remember Solly?

Typing a message>

Yes, of course I do. Goodbye, Harry dear.

"Oh, Rose, Rose, wake up. I was able to talk to Harry," said Doris. "This is so wonderful. How much do I owe you?

"You're my first customer for *HoneyI'mHome,* Doris, no charge today. Come back anytime, but better call me for an appointment, I think I'm going to be very busy."

So *HoneyI'mHome*.com became a great success, and much to the delight of her son, Al, Rose's income was on the rise. Oh, there were a few technical glitches like when Mrs. Studelman signed up to talk to Roger, and Roger turned out to be her late poodle. And when Mr. Enteman tried to serve a subpoena online to the late Everett Morgan, who had been his stockbroker, and who had lost a lot of money for him.

And sometimes there were other problems, as when Jimmy Rubin contacted his Uncle Syd and began to chew him out for not mentioning him in his will. Rose, still in her trance, woke up with a tremendous headache after the nasty messages floated back and forth through her.

In many instances her clients contacted the departed in order to find out something, blame somebody, confirm a suspicion, confess something, or just yell at them. Rose, as any good medium, was never part of the actual conversations, but the messages left a trail on her computer and she was able to print out what had transpired:

Typing a message>

Marvin, listen, I need you to tell me who to vote for...

Typing a message>

Fred dear, should I sell my Apple stock?

Typing a message>

Ethel, which laundry soap do we use in the washing machine?

Typing a message>

Ralph, I wanna know exactly what did happen on your last business trip to Elmira...

Typing a message>

Sure, Mona, I don't care if you remarry. Just don't let that guy loose in my wine cellar.

Typing a message>

Morty, can you clarify your suicide note for me. What did you mean, "enough is enough?"

Typing a message>

Dora, it's wonderful talking to you again. Is there any way you can sign a check?

***

Rose's son, Al, continued to tinker   and

improve *HoneyI'mHome.com*. Rose's business was doing great, but Al figured he could license the web site to other mediums like his mother. As word got out among other paranormal professionals, Rose's business grew and grew. Al sold pop-up advertising on the website to companies who marketed flowers, cemetery plots, investments, nursing homes, and more. Several investment companies wanted to take *HoneyI'mHome* public, and two years later the stock was traded on the New York Stock Exchange. "HIH."

Oh, there were a few competitors, but HIH, had a lock on the Spiritualist marketplace. Rose was often asked to be a speaker at conferences, paranormal, professional, and otherwise. When she spoke she gave a demo of HIH.com which always involved Sol, her late husband, who incidentally was on the Board of Directors and owned 30 percent of the stock. Rose put herself in a trance and her son, Al. set up a projector to show the messaging on a large screen.

Typing a message>

Solly dear, are you there? I'm speaking to important business people today. They want to meet you.

Typing a message>

Yes, I'm here Rose. Where else would I be? How's business?

Typing a message>

Fantastic Solly, we're all very rich.

Typing a message>

Nice, but fat lot of good it does me up here.

Typing a message>

But your grandkids will inherit big Solly.

Typing a message>

They should be well. Have them call me some time, Have Al call, too. Kids, they never call.

Listen Rose, I gotta go. Say hello to your important businessmen for me. Tell them Sol

Lieberman says hello.

Typing a message>

Goodbye for now, Solly.

Phil Braverman

CALL YOUR MOTHER!

I was waiting for my turn in the barber shop, reading a golf magazine, when I came across this really strange ad in the Personal Services section:

> *Can't bear to call your mother? We make those necessary and painful calls to your mom on a schedule you set. We make those calls you just dread making. Terrific results, happy moms, reasonable rates. Check out our services at: Callyourmother.com*

When I got home, I went straight to their web site. Here is how it works. First they send you a script. You read it back to them over the phone, and they record your voice. Now they have your voice print, and using their special software, their staff can make a call, and it will sound just like you! Wow, what a great idea, I thought I'd give it try. I entered my credit card information on their web site and signed up for a trial call for $4.95, a small price to pay if it worked. The very next day, my cell phone rang:

"Hello Mr. Gotnick, I'm Rachel from *Callyourmother.com*. I see from your e-mail signup you'd like the trial call to your mom. Welcome, and we're happy to have you as a client. I'm your personal representative and I'll be the one making the calls, using your voice. Can I call you Leonard?"

"Hi Rachel. Wow, this sounds exciting. So how do we get started? By the way, call me Lenny."

"Okay, Lenny. I'm going to e-mail you a list of words and phrases. We built this list from the profile you entered when you signed up. As soon as you get it we'll record the words on the list using your voice. Here we go, I'll hang on while you open your e-mail."

Lenny checks his inbox and sees an e-mail from Callyourmother.com. He opens it and lets Rachel know.

"Okay Lenny, when you're ready, go down the list and slowly speak the words and phrases into the phone as crisply as you can. It'll just take about five minutes. Got it?"

"Okay Rachel, I'm ready, here goes..."

Hi Ma, it's me, Lenny.

Yes Ma, I know it's late.

I'm sorry.

I'm very sorry!

How's Pa?

How's Aunt Sophie?

I'll try to do better next time.

I'm sorry I forgot your birthday.

I thought tomorrow was your birthday?

What do you want from me anyway?

Yes, I did eat today.

I'm full, I can't eat another bite.

I'll visit you over the holidays.

No, I don't date her anymore.

Nothing is wrong with my telephone finger.

Medical school is not for me.

I am dressing warmly.

No, she's not Jewish.

No, she's not married.

I didn't mean it that way.

Yes, I'll call you when the plane lands.

I can't come over for dinner.

I gotta hang up now, I hear someone at the door.

"Good job, Lenny! We'll enter your voice recording into our computer, then we'll do the trial call. I'll call using your voice and your mother will never know it's not you. I can fix it so you can listen in on the call. When's the best time for you tomorrow?"

"Any time after three pm, Rachel. That's when the stock market closes."

"Okay, I'll call you first and you can listen while I talk to her."

So on Thursday around 4:30 pm. Rachel called Lenny and then dialed Lenny's mom's number. Lenny could hear the phone ring and his mom answering. Rachel began the conversation using Lenny's voice:

"Hi Ma, it's me, Lenny."

"Hello, Leonard, I hardly recognize your voice anymore, do you have a cold?"

"I'm fine, really. I just called to find out how you are…"

"I'm okay, Leonard, the doctor says it's not serious."

"What doctor? What's going on"

"Just my regular checkup Leonard, that's all. Don't worry about me. Say, how is your job? Any promotions or raises you want to tell us about?"

"No, Ma, same-old, same-old. The hedge-fund business is kind of boring right now."

"I've never understood what you do Leonard. Is a hedge fund something like being a gardener? Why did you drop out of medical school?"

"Ma, I never went to medical school, how could I drop out? No, I am not a gardener, more like a stock broker."

"Your father and I never buy stocks, after what happened in the Depression. Say, do you need any money?"

"No, Ma, we're fine."

"Wait a minute, you said "we". Are you married and didn't tell us? Is it that Ruth person from the law firm I never liked?"

"No, Ma. I should have said "I'm" fine."

"Well, did you and Ruth break up?"

"There is no Ruth in my life right now."

"Then what is her name? Is she Jewish?"

"Ma, listen, I gotta go. How's Pa?"

"He's about the same, do you want to talk to him? I could wake him up."

"No, Ma, that's okay, just tell him I called."

"Will you be calling back?"

"Sure, Ma."

"Can I tell him what time you'll be calling back?"

"G'bye Ma. Say hello to Aunt Sophie."

"I wish I could dear, she died last week, you didn't know? Leonard? Lenny? ..."

Lenny listened in on the call and decided it was about as good a conversation as they ever had. He was really excited. He called Rachel again and signed up for the "call-a-week" plan.

So Lenny's mom, Minnie, got regular weekly calls from Rachel/Lenny. But after a month or so, she began to get suspicious, since Lenny never called her that often in his whole life.

One day on the bus she glanced at a magazine left on the seat and noticed the ad for *Callyourmother.com*. She smelled a rat! She confided in her nephew Martin (who is no big fan of Lenny). He advised her to get a new phone with Caller ID, and then she'd be able to see where Lenny's calls are really coming from. She did, and after the very next call from Lenny she called that number right back. Rachel answered. Minnie told her who she was, and told her that the jig was up!

"Oh, Mrs. Gotnik, I am so ashamed that you found out. Naturally, I will stop calling you immediately."

"Oh, no, dear, don't stop calling. It's so wonderful to hear from Lenny every week-- and the fact that he pays $19.95 a month just to talk to me, well it makes a mother proud. And by the way, now that you know so much about our family, what do you think of

Lenny?"

" *I think he's a very nice man to want to call his mother every week.*"

"He certainly is very nice, Dear, take a mother's word for it. Say, are you single?"

Phil Braverman

Family History

At the Campfire: Spring 2119

"Grandfather Eaglesbreath, tell us about the old ways of our People," said young Marvin Leftthewaterrunning to his Grandpa. He and his cousins were gathered around the campfire at the Awannee Hilton Hotel-Spa-Resort and Casino in Yosemite Valley, that glorious, but cool spring evening in 2119.

"Certainly, little Leftthewaterrunning. What would you like to know?"

"Grandfather, we want to hear stories about our ancestors, about the heroes, and the famous warriors, and the big battles they fought."

"All right children, I'll start with one of our most famous heroes. One that comes to mind immediately was born nearly 100 years ago. His name was Chef Who- Comes-From-Far-Out-But-Looks-Like-Us."

"Excuse me, Revered Grandfather," said Lester Threadbear; "you said *Chef*, don't you mean "Chief?"

"No, little Lester Threadbear, I mean Chef. It was Chef, Who-Comes-From-Far-Out-But-Looks-Like-Us who turned our casino restaurant into a Michelin Four Star establishment and bestowed great honor on our people, as well as bring in thousands of tourists, which translated into tons of cash."

"How did the restaurant get the four Michelin stars Grandfather?" said Paula Runningtab.

"Well, it's a great story, little Runningtab. Once upon a dark time, our casino restaurant served only ordinary food, along with a few California Indian recipes like acorn mush, which was frankly not a big seller, even among our own people. We searched among the local tribes for a better chef who could create a more delicious menu, as the other casinos in the area were eating our lunch, forgive the pun. Always remember, children, the key to a successful casino is good food, and in that regard, we were failing badly.

"We wanted a Native American Chef, of course, and we advertised in all the tribal magazines, but, that didn't work. We finally hired a headhunter, if you'll pardon the expression, and we got a good result, with one small exception. Instead of an American Indian Chef they found us an India Indian. Chef Babala Baasim. We said no, of course, but the head hunting agency convinced us that this guy was really good.

"So, we interviewed him. He was young and handsome and an awfully nice chap. He told us that his name in India means, 'One-Who-Smiles-From-Above.' At our request, he cooked dinner for the tribal elders and it was a knockout. He said he could cook many delicacies from his own country and put a Native American twist on them. It sounded good and we put it to the test with a mixed focus group of tribal folks and casino-goers.

"We asked him to work up a varied menu and cook for our focus group, and he did. It included Delhi Tanshposofa, Corn Soup-of-the-Three-Sisters-Bhopal. Pemmican and Prairie Turnips Bangalore style, Pemmican and Wild Rice Vindaloo, Bean and Corn Curry Stew, Mumbai Fish and Cattails, Chocolate Tortilla Fry Bread, Baked Sockeye Salmon, Jaipur Style, and lots of other dishes. They proved so delicious, we couldn't keep our test-tasters away from the buffet table.

"Well, let me tell you, children, his dishes hit a homerun. After a little discussion, we made him a salary offer he couldn't refuse. And then, after consulting the elders and some very deep thinking, we decided to ask him to be an honorary *MOT*, Member of the Tribe."

"How did that work?" said Alice Sittingduck. "Did he agree to do that?"

"Well, little Sittingduck, it was a tough

decision for him. He would have to change his name, and, of course, go through some of our tribal rites of passage. But he was lonely and missing his family, and I guess we seemed like family to him. He changed his name from Babala Bassim, to the one we gave him: Chef Who-Comes-From-Far-Out-But-Looks-Like-Us. The first thing he did was to shorten it to Chef Far-Out."

"So, Grandfather, you passed this guy off as a Native American, as a member of our tribe?" said Alice Sittingduck.

"Yes, it was easy, little Alice Sittingduck. He was dark skinned and looked sort of like us, but he talked a little funny--with a British accent, in fact. We hired the Berlitz people to work with him, and in a few months he sounded just like us. Chef Far-Out had a red spot on his forehead, a custom of his own tribe back home, but instead of asking him to remove it we had all the restaurant staff paint red spots on their foreheads before they came to work each day. So, he dressed like us, he looked like us and in a short time he talked like us. It was a major tribal victory. The other casinos never knew what hit them. The food he cooked up was outstanding. The restaurant began to get rave reviews and the casino business boomed and our tribe began to get rich.

"But, then the word got out and all of a sudden we had a problem. Several other casinos tried to hire our Chef away. We ended up promoting him to Chief Chef, with a bigger salary and a percentage of the restaurant gross. Then we sweetened the deal and offered him the pick of our prettiest girls as a wife. A small price to pay for what he was contributing to the tribe, wouldn't you say?"

"You mean you *GAVE* him a bride, Grandfather?" said Katrina Kosherhorse. "That's so gross."

"Well, Katrina Kosherhorse, it was completely voluntary. He checked out all our eligible young ladies but saw no one he liked, so we didn't press it. But then, by good fortune, he met my great grandniece, Marie Shoppingbear, who was home from college where she was studying for her MBA. They really hit it off and saw each other as often as possible. After she graduated and returned home, they married.

"Marie Shoppingbear was extremely bright and her new husband encouraged her to go to law school, which she did.

"After graduating law school and passing the State Bar, she convinced her husband that he was being a sucker for not getting better compensated for his significant contribution to the casino. Marie Shoppingbear immediately renegotiated his contract, and all of a sudden he owned 49 percent of the restaurant! But no matter, because we had just received our first Michelin star, and we were becoming internationally famous which allowed us to build this grand hotel and double the size of the casino. Our tribe prospered like never before, due to Chef Far-

Out and his team with the red dots on their foreheads."

"That is a great story, Grandfather," said Paula Runningtab. "No wonder we all drive Mercedes Benzs, and can afford to go to Stanford. But, Grandfather, what about some of our famous tribal warriors and the battles they fought. Who were they?"

"Let's save that for another night, little Paula Runningtab. Listen, young people, I'm getting a bit tired. I'd like a nightcap, and the Lounge Bar at our Hilton closes at Midnight. Goodnight, Children."

"Our Hilton? You mean we own the whole Hilton, Grandfather?" said Katrina Kosherhorse.

"Children, we own the whole Hilton Hotel Chain!"

"Goodnight, Grandfather Eaglesbreath," they called out in unison.

More Campfire Tales

"Grandfather Eaglesbreath, "said Jonathan Kneelingbear, "last time you told us about the great Chefs of our tribe of long ago. We want to know all about our famous tribal warriors."

"Yes, tell us about the great warriors," said Marvin Leftthewaterunning.

"Yes, yes, Children. I will begin with my great, grandniece, Marie Shoppingbear. She was our most famous lawyer."

"Grandfather," said Lester Treadbear, "don't you mean *warrior*? You said *lawyer*."

"No, no." said Eaglesbreath. "I mean lawyer. We stopped needing actual warriors long ago. But, we still had many big battles to fight. They were mostly about zoning, and tax battles, and other legal battles. So we had to have a staff of fierce lawyers.

"And my great grandniece, Marie Shoppingbear, was one of our very best. She negotiated some of our biggest battles: the battle for tribal land rights, the not-for-profit battles with the IRS, the battle over the gaming commission license, and the battle for the oil and mineral rights on our Sacred Burial Mountain."

"What was the most famous battle of all, Grandfather?"

"Well, of course, our most famous battle was The Battle of the Bands."

"You mean a battle between the tribal Bands?" said Alice Sittingduck.

"No, I mean the battle of the biggest of the Big Bands – the battle to determine who owned the rights to have Tony Bennett and his band exclusively at their casino. A hugely important episode in our tribal history."

"Tell us about that, Grandfather," said Alice Sittingduck.

"Yes, my child. By the time that battle was

fought, Mr. Bennett was already 105 years old, but still going strong. As all you children know, entertainment is very important in running a successful casino, and in those days the biggest entertainer of them all was Tony Bennett. He sang, "I Left My Heart in San Francisco."

"Where is San Francisco, Grandfather?" said Katrina Kosherhorse.

"It is on a great bay, Katrina Kosherhorse, about 150 miles from our home here in Yosemite. One of our subsidiaries, the Alcatraz band of Indians runs the City these days and we own the biggest casino in the Bay Area.

"To continue: as the legend goes, Tony Bennett packed them in at every venue he played. When he sang at the casinos, both Indian and the ones in Vegas and Atlantic City, their business boomed. That was our experience too.

"Our wise tribal elders decided, because of

the connection to our San Francisco casino, he should sing only for us. If we could obtain his contract, we could be assured of success as long as he lived, and he did live to be over 118 years old. The oldest person on earth, and certainly the oldest living gravel-throated nightclub entertainer.

"The question was: how could we get his contract? We put our best minds on the case and learned that his current contract was held by the Mafia, the Five Families. Have you heard of them, children?"

"Yes, Grandfather, they are bad guys! Do they still control entertainment at many casinos?"

"Not anymore, Paula Runningtab.

"Our tribal leaders asked Marie Shoppingbear, now a famous lawyer in her own right, to take on the effort, and make the Mafia and Tony Bennett an offer they could not refuse. She got right to work and contacted Tony's agent.

"Tony, it seems, was very interested. We offered him a gold plated microphone, all you can eat spaghetti at the buffet, and promised we would make him an honorary tribal member. And, we promised he could sing at our San Francisco casino, which, by then, took up, with parking spaces, most of the first six blocks of the Golden Gate Park. Tony accepted. It was easy--a piece of Indian fry bread, as we say. Tony did not give a hoot about money at that point, being 105 and all. He had buckets of money. What he cared about most was being able to sing to his fans in his beloved City by the Bay.

"Now, the Mafia, who held his contract, that's another story altogether. They saw it another way. Tony was their bread and butter in their Entertainment Division, and Marie Shoppingbear had quite a job on her hands. But, and you should know this children, the Indian Nations, flush with casino cash had been moving in on the Mafia for years. Our National Tribal Council had already bought out the lotto business, the sanitation business, olive oil distribution, sewer cover manufacturing, Pizza Restaurants, and their port operations. Weary of all this, and with many of their members "retiring" the Mafia bosses were open to negotiation. It is written in stone (and also secretly tape recorded) that the negotiations went like this:

"So, Marie Shoppingbear." said Luigi *Bononcini, head of the Entertainment Division of the Mafia. "You come to us asking to buy out Tony Bennett's contract. Is that what we are hearing?"*

"Yes, Mr. Bononcini, we are going to make you an offer you can't refuse."

"I have to laugh. Don't we, fellows? That is what we usually say."

"Well, now the moccasin is on the other foot, Luigi. May I call you Luigi? asked Marie.

"What could you possibly offer us that we don't already own, or could easily steal?" asked Luigi.

"Luigi," said Marie. "my tribe owns, as an

investment, six beautiful villages in Southern Italy. We happened to know they are the villages your Capos, your top bosses, come from. You can have these towns in exchange for Tony's contract."

"Well, I don't know," said Luigi.

"Listen to me carefully, Luigi," said Marie, "I am only going to say this once. Tony is only 105 now, and wouldn't it be a shame if he had an 'accident' and couldn't sing anymore while you still had his contract?"

"Yes, that would be a real shame. When you say you own these towns, what exactly do you mean?"

"We own every thing. The buildings, the water company, the post office, the bakeries, the local police. It is all legitimate, too. You can have your lawyers look at the property deeds and the secret video recordings of our handshakes with the police and local politicians. What more could you want for proof?"

"Let me talk to my people. Your offer sounds attractive and we are getting a bit tired of hearing

Tony sing at our weddings, funerals, and annual meetings. If you throw in your fishing rights in the State of Montana, I think we may have a deal."

"So it came to pass, little Sittingduck. that the Tribe bought out Tony Bennett's contract. He and his band headlined at the Golden Gate Park Casino for 13 more years before he made that final trip to that sweathouse on the Sacred Mountain (where incidentally much oil and gas had been found). During his time with us, our casinos prospered and our tribe became wealthy beyond description. We bought back much of our tribal land in San Francisco from Google and Facebook. And, Marie Shoppingbear was promoted to Chief Lawyer and given many honors. She became a legend and it turns out she could sing too. For many years she accompanied Tony on stage, to great audience applause.

"And that, children, is the story of our most famous lawyer, and our biggest battle: The Battle of the Bands."

"That is a wonderful story, Grandfather,

please tell us another. Tell us about the battle with the IRS. Did we win that one?"

"Yes, and no, Katrina Kosherhorse. But that is a story for another evening by the campfire. Now, children, go on back to your suites at our Awannee Hilton Hotel, and Sweet Dreams."

"Goodnight, Grandfather Eaglesbreath!"

Myra and Morris

In the last seconds before they both passed, Myra and Morris, married just short of 70 years, were given the choice, by a heavenly spirit (who identified himself only as Hershel Wachter, Heavenly Spirit), of an eternity on a cruise ship, or an indefinite stay the Marcelo Resort and Spa in Puerto Vallarta. Myra opted for the cruise ship mainly because most times Mexican food repeated on her a few hours after eating. Besides, she had friends who would be envious of her living on a fancy cruise ship. Morris, of course, went along with her decision as he always did.

The couple were now in their verandah cabin suite with a view, playing gin rummy.

"Morris, I was just thinking of that experience last week with Barry and the kids. We really should have told them more about your folks and my folks in the old country and how they got over here, well, down there, I mean" said Myra.

"It's your turn to deal, I'll cut the cards," said Morris.

"Morris, are you listening to me?"

"Of course I am, I'm always listening. Now deal, please."

"Tell me again about your family in Russia," said Myra.

"What's to tell? They were poor, they were persecuted, they saved their money and they left. They came here, they did well End of story."

"C'mon, Morris, you can do better than that."

"Well, my grandpa Max was a shoemaker for the Tsar's army post in his village. He would make new boots for the officers and repair their old ones. When the soldiers would come in they would talk to each other about where they were going to be sent. Grandpa would write down that information and later pass it on to whomever the Tsar was fighting that month. They would pay him for the information, of course."

"You mean, he was a spy?"

"Well, I understand he thought of himself in the

information services business."

"Wasn't that risky?"

"It was more risky if he made a pair of boots that didn't fit. Everybody sold secrets; it was the most popular industry in his village."

"Between the boots and the sale of military information, Max was able to buy a cow for the family. They lived pretty well, if you like cheese. Later, he found he could sell the same military information to both sides. The Russians even gave him a medal. He bought another cow, and another. Soon there was enough money for him and grandma and their three children to take the boat to New York. So, after he made them each a new pair of shoes, because you never knew, they set sail for America. That's what I know about the old country."

"Well," said Myra." What happened to Max and his family when they got here and what year was that?"

"I think it was 1902. Max was in his early 30's. He worked for a boot manufacturer for awhile and then started his own company. Then the U.S.

government found out about his spying talents in the old country and used him as an agent. They sent him back to Russia to find out what was going on with those revolutionaries. He was disguised as the valet to the U.S. Trade Ambassador. At the Moscow trade conference center, when all the valets were in the basement cleaning the shoes of their ambassadors, he learned the dates of the planned October Revolution. This information he passed on to Washington and many American businessmen were warned to get out of Russia before all hell broke loose. For this he was given a medal by President Wilson."

"The family never knew about this? I never knew!"

"He was a modest man, Max. His wife thought he was in Argentina buying leather for boots."

"Oh, my goodness. So Max was an American hero? Our kids would die to hear this. Well, not die. Go on, then what did he do?"

"Then when Prohibition began he went from spying and making boots, to spying and bootlegging. He was a double agent for the Feds, and because they couldn't ever break his cover and give him a medal, they let him keep the profits from his bootlegging operation. In return, he informed on the Mafia's bootlegging activities; a dangerous business. But, after Prohibition ended, Grandpa Max was a wealthy man and invested in a chain of shoe stores. By that time, my father, Marvin, Max's only son, joined the firm. After Max retired, he became CEO and the business grew into the Sole Bros Shoe Fair chain of stores."

"I knew your father worked for a shoe company. But CEO? Then, how come we weren't wealthy? How come we lived in that old house in that small town in the Midwest."

"We were very rich, Myra. Very rich. You just forgot. And, that was your folk's house we moved to. You just wanted to live there. We could have lived anywhere. Anywhere. After Dad passed, I took over the Sole Bros chain for years until we sold it to Nike for $300 million dollars."

"Oh, yeah, that's right, I do remember that. We did have some money. Your father, Marvin, was he a spy too?"

"No, but he did important war work. His company made shoes for the Women's Army Corps. And he was an inventor. He invented the portable shoe tree, orthotic inserts, and Velcro for people who couldn't tie their shoes. He's in the Shoe Manufacturers' Hall of Fame in Shoefalls, South Dakota. Do you remember going there?"

"Say, Morris. Is all this stuff really true or are you just making it up for the kids?"

"Who knows? Family stuff. This was all your idea."

"But, we were rich right? Tell me again how rich we were."

"It's your turn to cut the cards and deal, Myra."

Myra's Story

"So, Myra, now you know about my grandfather in the old country. How about your people? You never talk much about them. I know they came from Russia too. Were they horse thieves, smugglers, what?" said Morris from his deck chair on the luxury cruise ship, Eternal Princess of the Sea. "So, spill the beans. We're both dead. I got all afternoon."

"Here's what I was told, Morris," said Myra. "I was told my grandma Moira was a music hall singer in London. Her family got there from Russia, smuggled in a shipping container full of herring when she was just a little girl. She was raised in Tottenham, the Russian area of London. She grew up speaking Russian but she was very smart and soon learned good English. In school she sang in the choir with a beautiful voice, and became a professional singer. First, she sang at pubs, then she sang at those British music halls which were so popular at the end of the century.

"So, there she was in Piccadilly, singing and

earning a living at it, too. Then, when she was 18, she had an opportunity to sail to the States to be in a production of HMS Pinafore. You know the opera with all those British sailors? But when she got off the boat she found the opera was already playing in New York!"

"No!" said Morris. "What happened?"

"Well, the production was secretly copied in London and stolen from it's authors Gilberg and Sillverman, I think. This was before the copyright laws, my mother told me."

"Then what did she do?" asked Morris. "Imagine your poor young grandmother all alone in New York and out of work."

"Not a lot she could do. Some relatives in New York got her a job as a chicken plucker at a kosher butcher. Her job was to remove all the feathers from the chickens. The chickens were dead first, of course. Some job for a trained singer, huh!

"It turned out that the butcher, Sol, had a son, Sam, and after Sam took his apron off in the evening and washed his hands, he didn't look so bad. So she married him. They were married for two years, but then things went wrong."

"So, what happened with Sam?"

"Grandma got so she just couldn't stand the sight of meat and blood and chicken feathers anymore. And, just looking at Sam everyday with his bloody apron on made her sick to her stomach. So, she became a vegetarian, quit the butcher shop, and went to work at Ralph Jaffe's vegetable stand next door. Sol and Sam were furious, partially because they never paid her a salary after the marriage, and now they would actually have to hire somebody. And partly because they felt it was a sin in those days not to eat meat when it was available."

"I can understand that," said Morris.

"So, Grandma took what little money she had managed to save and hopped a train for San Francisco where she hoped for a better life. When she got there, remember, Morris, she was a professional singer, she saw an ad for an opening for a dinner singer at the Grand Palace Hotel dining room. There she met Enrico Caruso, who was 33 at the time, and she dated him for a few months. He was playing Don Jose in Carmen at the opera house and staying at the Palace, his favorite hotel. Rico would have been a good catch, even being Italian and all, don't you think, Morris?"

"So, then?"

"So, just then the 1906 earthquake happened and there was panic and destruction big time. Grandma lost her job and her boyfriend, as Rico fled the City never to return. Poor Grandma, what could she do? After the dust settled, Grandma ended up plucking chickens again at the Chrystal Palace Market, newly reopened among her ruins. You'd think she'd have learned a lesson, but she ended up marrying the chicken seller, Mendel, my grandfather. After a year they moved to Petaluma to become chicken ranchers.

"But it was a good marriage and together they opened an operatic chicken restaurant called Your Chicken, the first of several successful operatic chicken restaurants they owned. He was the cook; mostly chicken. She served the chicken and sang for the customers; mostly arias."

"Then what happened?"

"Well, my mother, Marsha, was born of course. She grew up on their ranch but had no interest in raising chickens or opera singing. She was a good student and the first in the entire family to go to college. She went to college in Berkeley and majored in business. Then she went back to Petaluma and helped her parents expand Your Chicken to more than a dozen restaurants, all up and down the West Coast.

"It was in LA where my mom met her husband, my father. They met at a restaurant owners' convention. He and his parents owned a chain of successful Chinese restaurants called Wong's Kosher Kitchens.

"They fell in love, got married, and myself and my brother, Al, soon came along. We both grew up working around the restaurants. The families soon merged the two chains and the names. Your Chicken and Wong's Kosher became Your Wong: Chinese Kosher Cuisine.

"And when I grew up, I met you in Men's Shoes. You know the rest of the story."

"Interesting. So, Myra, tell me about your great grandfather in England. What did he do before he left Russia?"

"Let's talk later, Morris. Time to go to dinner. I think I'll have the chicken."

Fivel of Russia and London

"Myra," said Morris, in between bites of a chicken wing. So what more do you know about your Grandma Moria's father, your great grandfather?"

"I know only a little bit. His name was Fivel. I think he made some good money after he got to London. I was told that he paid for my grandmother's trip to New York. I also heard he was unhappy with her wanting to be a singer. He wanted her to run a Russian Tea Room and Betting Parlor. Beyond that I know very little. Finish your chicken, Morris."

"That's not a lot of information about him, Myra. I think I'll get a box for the rest of this chicken."

"Well, now that I think about it, Morris," said Myra, "why don't we just ask him? He's long dead too, and I got a hunch he picked the Marcelo, Puerto Vallarta, Mexico Resort as his after-life option. Grandma always said he liked to fish."

"So, Myra, how on earth, (oops, sorry) are we going to contact him?"

"That's easy. Sol Lieberman. You know Sol, from shuffleboard? Sol's wife, Rose, is still living. She's a Medium and runs a Spirit Shop, I think it's called *Honey, I'm Home.com.* It's high tech spiritualism, using a web site her son built to help her connect to the dead. Sol runs the dead end of the business. He can probably link us up to my great grandpa, Fivel."

You should know that Madam Rose Lieberman, MP (Master in Parapsychology), connects, for a reasonable fee, her living clients with their dearly departed. But, she had never dealt with connecting two departed clients. So, Sol's request to his wife to connect two dead people was a little out of the ordinary, even for her. But, Rose was up to the challenge. After signing on to the Spirit Computer System, and with the help of her late husband Sol, she was able to enter into her usual trance and complete the connection.

Sol Lieberman and Fivel are now connected on a ghostly-looking video screen.

"Hey, Fivel," said Sol. "This is Sol, Sol Lieberman. Are you out there? We know you're at the Marcelo Resort in Mexico. Your great granddaughter, Myra, wants a word with you. My wife Rose can connect you, no charge."

"How is Myra?" said Fivel. "Have you seen her? She must be quite old by now"

"Pretty dead, Fivel. She and her husband Morris took the Cruise Ship Afterlife Option, like I did. She has questions for you. Family stuff."

"Oh, okay, tell your wife, Rose, I guess she can connect us. Can't stay too long though, almost dinner time here."

Fivel and Myra are now connected: grainy, ghostly figures on Sol's screen, but better than nothing.

"Hello, Myra my dear. What a nice surprise. So you're my daughter Moira's granddaughter! You look just like your grandmother, only dead. What can I do for you, sweetie?"

"Well, great grandpa, I heard about you from Grandma Moira and my mother, Marsha, but they only knew a little bit. I want to know about your life in Russia, before you moved to London. What did you do in Russia--in the old country?"

"Oh, that," said Fivel, "I had odd jobs here and there. For awhile I was a ghost writer for Leo Tolstoy. You know the Peace and War guy? Leo called me up one day. 'Fivel,' he said, 'this goddamn book I'm working on is getting way too long. Can you take over for a few chapters? I need to visit my cousin Melvin in Pinsk?' I said, 'sure, Leo, I'll help. You go visit Melvin.' So, I wrote seven chapters of War and Peace. You'd have thought he would have mentioned me. No, the cheap bastard didn't even send me a copy."

"What else did you do, Great Grandpa? "You said you had other odd jobs?"

"Well, I was boot maker to the Tsar. I knew your husband's grandfather too, when he was very young and just getting started making soldiers' boots, and spying. We shopped at the same leather store. I made the Tsar's riding boots and his slippers too. Small feet. I think he and Napoleon could have exchanged shoes for Christmas if they weren't always fighting. The Tsar, Nick, he liked the boots, he liked me. I became his food taster to make sure nobody put poison in his food. If someone tried to poison him; zap, that would be me. Nick trusted me and promoted me from taster to food watcher in the kitchen, to watch that the food taster should not put poison in his Stochamoiitscha."

"So, go on, Great Grandpa, we heard you made some money when you got to London. You weren't poor like a lot of the immigrants. How'd that happen?"

"Eggs, that's how I made my money. Eggs."

"You mean you had lots of chickens?"

"Chickens, schmickens. Well we had a few of those too, but there's no money in chickens. I'm talking about Faberge eggs—have you ever seen one? Beautiful! After I left my job at the Tsar's Palace, I got a job at the Faberge factory in Moscow where they made those beautiful jeweled eggs. The Tsar gave me a good recommendation and I was put in charge of egg polishing."

"One evening as I was cleaning up to go home, I found the door to the vault left open and I just helped myself to some of those eggs, thinking I would take a little polishing work home with me and get ahead on the job. They were so beautiful, my wife went nuts when she saw them. So, we decided to keep two eggs. All of our neighbors in the shetl were very impressed."

"Didn't the factory notice the eggs had gone missing?"

"They didn't notice, they made so many eggs. And besides, the Tsar was always helping himself to the eggs. I think they lost count. This happened again a few months later, and before you know it, I had an even dozen Faberge eggs which I kept in a jumbo egg carton. I knew they were beautiful but I learned they were very valuable too—who knew? So, I got a little worried and decided to leave Russia before they found me out. A few months later, and with the money we made selling our live chickens, I moved the family to London."

"How did you get the eggs into the country?"

"That was easy. You know those little Russian dolls, the ones that are nested one inside each other? That's how the eggs came in, inside a dozen dolls. Believe me, the custom's man was not interested in inspecting any more of those stupid dolls."

"Wow, did you sell the eggs when you got to London?"

"Had to. I applied to be a food taster to the

Royal Family, but the Union of Royal Tasters had a long wait list. It seemed very few of their union members had been poisoned during the current reign. Then the money from the sale of chickens ran out. I knew I had to sell an egg or two."

"How did you find a buyer? You must have known what you were doing was a little on the shady side."

"Shady, schmady. Times were tough. There was no eBay then, so I had be creative. At the time there were lots of private, wealthy collectors who I heard would love to get their hands on one of those eggs. So I very carefully advertised in the food section of the London Times:

Fresh eggs, very tasty, brown and white. Some with jewels. Reasonably priced. Call Gooch 234. Will deliver.

"That ad brought me my first customer, Philo de Mony, a Count. He bought an egg from me."

"How much did you get for it?"

"I don't remember exactly, five maybe six pounds. That was good money in those days. You could buy a flat in Mayfair for 10 pounds. For 20 pounds you could buy a soccer team."

"Wow. Did the family and your neighbors know you had that kind of money?"

"No, we didn't advertise. But later they found out I owned half the Manchester United soccer team."

"You owned Manchester United? Morris, did you hear that?"

"Just for three seasons, including one World Cup championship. After that I sold my share and invested in a betting parlor and tea room. You know, I think I may still have an egg or two somewhere. I'll have to ask my new wife Yolanda Celine if she's seen it."

"Gee, Great Grandpa Fivel, if you find it will you let Morris and me know? Maybe we can arrange to see it?"

"Sure, sweetie. Listen, I have to end this and go to dinner now. It's Mexican Night. They're having Huevos Rancheros at the Marcelo. Love those eggs. But, feel free to call back any time."

"So nice talking to you, Great Grandpa! Love to Yolanda Celine."

"Thanks for doing this Sol," said Myra. Thank Rose for us too."

"I will. Goodbye Fivel. Stay well," said Sol. Bye, Myra. Bye, Morris. Always nice to see you both looking so good."

Phil Braverman

The Family Business

Grandma Ruth's Auto Laundry and Bagel Shoppe

Ruth Gilson lost her husband in May of 2009. I mean she really lost him. They were at Costco shopping for a Friday night roasted chicken and he wandered off; never to be seen again. She suspected a kidnap but there was never a ransom note. Besides who would want Bernard: 78 years old, overweight, with very little hair, false teeth and a schlub of a dresser to boot? Actually, Ruth didn't much want him either and she was quite relieved. In deference to her missing husband, she did not shop again at that same Costco except for the first few weeks, when she went to see if anybody had turned him in to the lost and found. They hadn't, and finally she left her phone number with the office and that was that.

Of course a missing-persons form was filled out, but the police gave her little hope; about as much chance as finding a TV stolen from an apartment after a break-in. After awhile everybody stopped looking, and Bernard was declared expired by the insurance company. Ruth had no fat husband, but instead, a big fat check.

A year or two went by and Ruth began to get a bit bored. She thought perhaps it was time to do something. She figured she was too old to get a job. Volunteer work, although fun, left a lot of time on her hands. Perhaps buying a business would work, she thought. Despite her age, she still had a lot of energy. Before Bernard retired he owned a small waffle-cone manufacturing company. Ruth did the books and she knew how to run a business.

So she watched the Want Ads, the Business Opportunities section, and one day found this

Ad:

It looked perfect! An old fashioned car wash, high end vehicles, simple operation, no merchandise (*although that might well   ,* she thought). After suitable inquiries she met the owner at the car wash. It was only about 3 miles from her house. And another plus, they hit it off great.

"Why are you selling?" Ruth asked.

"Retiring," was the answer. "I'm a widower and I want to spend more time with my grandchildren and do some traveling."

Perfect, thought Ruth, *and he's kind of cute too.* She inspected the place with him and found the car wash immaculate, the equipment highly polished and obviously well cared for (although there was a little dust on the office window sills). Needs a woman's touch, she thought.

After a formal inspection by safety people and an engineer, Ruth made an offer which was quite acceptable to Gordon *(they were on first name terms by then).* They worked out a schedule in which she could train for 30 days and then take over the car wash. "I've a lot of good ideas," Ruth told Gordon. "Not that you've neglected the place, just some new thinking."

First, a new name would be appropriate. The current name, *Gordon's Quick Auto Bath*, didn't do it for her. *Grandma Ruth's Auto Laundry and Bagel Shoppe*, was the name she picked. About the bagels, she reasoned that if people are here waiting for their cars, they should eat a bagel. So she contracted to add a small coffee shop counter in the office, serving bagels with or without cream cheese, and coffee or tea. Nothing fancy, she felt the food inspectors might get upset with a more lavish menu at a car wash (given all the machinery, soapm and dirty water and such).

When she took over, the signs around the car wash yard, read: *Please leave the keys in the car. Shut all the windows. Don't leave the engine running. Remove all valuables. Don't enter the wash area.*

Ruth thought: *It's a new day, we should have some new rules and some new signs.* These are the signs she had made up and posted around the car wash:

For Customers:

- *Never park under a tree*
- *Please rinse off your car before you come to the car wash*
- *While you are waiting, call your mother!*
- *If you use our restroom, it's a good time to brush your teeth*
- *While you are waiting, you stay out of the sun*
- *You should always buckle up when leaving the car wash*

For Employees:

- *All employees must wash hands before washing cars*
- *Always use a clean towel when wiping the car*
- *Do the older ladies' cars first*

- *Offer a toll house cookie when handing them the car key*
- *Say "you really shouldn't have," when accepting a tip*
- *Give them a hug and offer them another cookie*
- *Ask when they are coming back, get a specific date*
- *Give them our number, ask them to call*
- *Always wave goodbye*

Grandma Ruth herself was very good with customers.

"Hello Dear. Welcome to my car wash. How can I help you, Dear?"

"I'd like a car wash please."

"What's your name, Dear?"

"Frank, ma'am."

"Frank, that's a nice name. I had an uncle Frank. A wonderful man but he drank. You don't drink too much do you?"

"No ma'am, just some beer now and then."

"Stop the ma'am stuff, Frank, please call me Grandma Ruth."

"Is that your car over there? Lovely car. It's not German is it?"

"No, ma'am, er, Grandma Ruth."

"Is it paid for? You must have a good job, thank God. Are you married? Listen, have a bagel while you're waiting for your car. I'll call my sister Ida. Her daughter, my beautiful niece Sophie, might like to come over and meet you."

"So, Frank, that will be $19.50. $18 for the car wash and $1.50 for the bagel. The coffee is on the house. Oh, I see you have a Diamond MasterCard. Sophie is gonna like that. Here's your receipt. Thank you, dear. Come back soon."

Ruth's business prospered. On many days there were quite a few cars waiting in line for a wash and a bagel. One day a blue Ford sedan drove in for a wash. The driver checked in at the counter.

"Ruth? Is that you?"

"Bernard!" she screamed! "Where have you been? We thought you were dead! What happened to you at Costco, where did you go?"

"I followed this lady out of the store, she looked just like you. I thought it was you. Her name is Ruth, too. She took me home. She's a great cook and lets me eat what I want and wear what I want. I thought it would be best for everyone if I just stayed with her."

"My God, Bernard, you can't just disappear like that! You left me alone with not even a goodbye."

"Sorry, Ruth, but the other Ruth, she's a wonderful cook and she doesn't nag about the way I dress. But it's a rotten shame you have to work in a car wash at your age."

"No, Bernard, I own this place and it's very successful, no thanks to you!"

"Gee, Ruth. That's nice."

"So Bernard, I guess if you're happy with the new Ruth, then you're happy. I met someone too, his name is Gordon, he used to own this place. We're a couple now. But tell me one thing Bernard."

"What's that, Ruth?"

"Would you like the regular wash or the deluxe wash?"

My Aunt Betty's Duck

On a recent visit to Aunt Betty she told me the story of the duck that changed her life. I recorded our conversation and maybe you'd like to hear what she said. It was a pretty fantastic story.

"Well, Denise, when I was just a little girl, maybe eight or nine, a family friend gave me a baby duckling he'd won at a carnival. I loved that duckling. I named him (or her, I never really knew) Fuzzy, after my security blanket, long in shreds by then. As the months passed and Fuzzy grew, he (I'll call him, he, from now on) followed me everywhere; to school, to the library. and to the playground, despite there being threatening dogs and little boys with sticks. Fuzzy grew fat, very fat.

"Well, we were very poor (did I ever tell you that, Denise?) and one day when I came down from my room for dinner, I smelled the most delicious aroma from the kitchen. It turned out to be Fuzzy in the oven!

"I screamed at my parents and I was devastated,

and shed many tears, needless to say. But, then I calmed down and the fact was I was hungry, like the rest of the family. So I dug in. Fuzzy was delicious. I'd never tasted anything so good before, and the fact that he was my best friend made it even more special."

"How old were you when you ate Fuzzy, Aunt Betty?"

"I guess I was 11 or 12 by the time. Old enough to go back to the carnival, which was back in town that summer, and buy two more ducklings: Florence and Edgar. I decided by that time I'd raise ducks for a living when I grew up and, well, why wait?

"Florence and Edgar grew fast. Although they became good friends, like Fuzzy, it was their eggs I was really after, and they didn't disappoint. They laid enough eggs to eat a few and sell the rest. I used the money to buy more ducks. By the time I was in high school, I had dozens of ducks, hundreds of eggs to sell, and lots of delicious duck dinners with my family. Too bad you weren't around in those days, Denise."

"Wow, you had a food business when you were in high school?"

"It was duck soup easy, honey. By the time I graduated, I was selling ducks, fresh and frozen, to all the restaurants and butcher shops in town. And, fresh eggs to the grocery stores. My ducks were known all over the nearby counties for their freshness and taste. I was going to name the business Fuzzy Ducks, but saying that sounds like something that might get stuck in your throat. So Betty's Ducks it was. Then I borrowed some money and I opened a restaurant specializing in duck dinners. I named it Duck Queen and we served Roast Duck, Duck a l' Orange, Peking Duck, Twice Cooked Duck, Piri-Piri Duck, Shredded Duck and weekly specials. Business was fantastic. We opened in several other towns (I had a business partner by then) and we sold Duck Queen franchises all around the country. The DQ franchise became very valuable."

"Excuse me, Aunt Betty. Didn't Dairy Queen have a problem with that?"

"Now that you mention it, Denise, they had a big problem. They sued us and we had to either drop the DQ branding or buy them out. We dropped the DQ cause I didn't want to buy them and mess with their restaurants. Besides I was working on my first cookbook: *Everyday Duck.* The book was a huge seller as were my next books, *Everybody Duck!!* and *Quack Snacks.* I did a show on the Food Network for awhile called *Quackers.* Denise, do you know how many ways you can prepare duck?"

"No, Aunt Betty, lots I guess."

"Not that many actually. And, that kind of put a limit on my cooking show programming. Oh, of course I could have done goose or pigeon or quail or pheasant, but I remained loyal to Fuzzy, my former best friend. So, I gave up the TV show. But, the guest appearances on the Today show, the Tonight show, and book signings kept me very busy. And besides that, I traveled around the world looking for new ways to fix duck. Never found many though.

"I was in my early 40's by then, and getting a bit bored with the whole business of duck. I felt it was time to move on. So, I sold the business to Exxon/Mobil, and I pocketed a ton of cash and stock. That's how you could afford that fancy Ivy League college, Denise. I bet your parents never told you, did they? Jerks! Anyway, I decided to start another business. I remembered we used to feed the ducks fishmeal among other things, and it was very expensive. I decided to go into the fish products business. I started with just a few fish, just like the ducks and before long, my company, Go Fish, owned fish farms, fish and chips shops, frozen fish finger manufacturing, and tropical fish stores. And the fishmeal business, of course. I stayed away from fish sauce—too salty."

"Wow, Aunt Betty, you were some kind of business woman! Then what happened?"

"Much the same story, Denise. I opened a chain of restaurants called, Something Fishy. And I wrote a series of cookbooks you may have seen. *Fishbones Without Fear, Tails from the Sea,* and *Betty Cooks Huckleberry Fins.* All very successful. But I got bored again. I sold Go Fish, to Shell Oil and made another packet. That's what put you through medical school. Of course, those idiot parents of yours didn't tell you, did they?"

"I suspected you did, Aunt Betty. Then what did you do?"

"My next venture had nothing to do with ducks or fish or restaurants or cookbooks. I went into the solar panel business."

"No way!"

"I bought a business that did solar technology, built panels and storage and control units. It came with an exclusive franchise and legal rights to the sunniest place on earth, the Equator. But, that's another long story. Listen, Denise, it's been great seeing you. We have to do this again. Before you go, can I make you a sandwich? I have some cold roast duck which is pretty tasty."

"Thanks, Aunt Betty, I'm a vegetarian these days."

"Well how about some fish, can you eat fish?"

Well that's the story of my Aunt Betty's duck. Aunt Betty recently moved to Las Vegas. I had a postcard from her recently. She opened a new chain of restaurants called Burger Queen."

That's My Dad!

My father is a bird. No, really, I'm not kidding. Ralph, that's my Dad, died almost 10 years ago and he was reincarnated, first as a cat. Then he died again, after choking on a fish bone. Next, he came back as a goldfish but his owner overfed him. After that, he lived as a squirrel for awhile until a Prius got him. And finally, he came back as a redwing blackbird.

My daughters and I bumped into him about six months ago at Costco where, and you may have trouble believing this, he works as a security guard in the loss-prevention department. I'm not making this up. Moreover, he got married and his wife Leslie works there too. Leslie is very nice, she's also a redwing blackbird. She was a concert pianist in her former life. I hadn't visited Dad for awhile, and that day I was going to Costco to see if he's still worked there.

"Hi, I'm looking for my father, Ralph," I said to the sales associate, "you know Ralph, the bird? He works in Security."

"I think he's in today. Should be in his office," he said.

"Office?"

"Yes, Ralph's head of Store Security, now. He was promoted last month."

"Oh my goodness. Can I see him?" I said. "I'm his son!"

"Oh, you must be Eric. He talks about you. Funny you don't look like him, not much family resemblance."

"Yes, Dad's a bird now. But he wasn't always a bird. It's a long story."

"Okay, Eric, you can go in now I'm sure he'll be happy to see you."

Enters Ralph's office

"Hi, Dad."

"Eric!" he said. "Good to see you again, Boy." "How are those beautiful daughters of yours? Philomena and Erica wasn't it?"

"No, Dad, Morwenna and Petula. Say, when I came looking for you they said you'd been promoted to head of security. How the heck did that happen?"

"Well Son, we were having a major crime wave here at the store and I solved it. Leslie helped too."

"How is Leslie?" I asked.

"Oh, she's great. She's only working part time now that I've been promoted. The rest of the time she spends redecorating our nest. We have several, a condo nest with a view of Lake Tahoe which you might like, and one at the beach. Do you still like the beach?"

"Wow,Dad, it sounds like you've become

very successful," I said. "Can you talk about the crime wave you solved that got you promoted?"

"Sure, Eric, but keep it under your hat. You see we were losing mattress sets right and left in the store. Now you'd think it would be very hard to steal mattresses but believe you me, it was happening. I was asked by my boss to find out what the heck was going on."

"So for days Leslie and I did a stakeout up in the rafters above the mattress displays. We had a bird's eye view,of course, and my Leslie has eyes like a…well, she has excellent vision. Finally we spotted a couple of bad apples doing what looked like re-labeling the goods. Turns out they were using a re-labeler they bought from some sleazebag outfit called 'Trader Tom's.' They were relabeling the item tags as "Air Mattresses" at a price of $19.95. At the checkout, the staff saw the word "mattresses" when they scanned the items and just let the system do the rest, you know how busy our cashiers are.

"The same thing happened when those bad birds left the building with the mattresses, the staff who checks the items in your cart on the way out saw the word mattress on the receipt and didn't look at the price, and why should they? We lost $85,000 worth of stock in two months before I solved the crime. Those scumbag perps are now awaiting trail for 'grand theft mattress' which carries a 5 year sentence. Do you know they also pulled off the "do-not-remove" tags just to be funny. They sang like canaries when they were arrested, and they confessed to those thefts. I hope they have to sleep on hard cots in the slammer. But anyway, it was a career-changer for me, that's one good thing."

"Wow, Dad, that's quite a story. No wonder they promoted you."

"So now," he said, "as head of security, I get to be in on all the meetings with the rest of store management. You do remember I was a marketing executive in my human life. I've got some great ideas to increase sales. I'm working up a Power-Point presentation for next week for some new products. I'll let you know how it goes."

"That's fantastic Dad. Well, I guess you're really busy. Hugs and pecks or whatever, to Leslie. I've got to go pick up my roasted chicken and a few other things...gee, Dad, I hope you're not upset about us eating chicken, you being a bird yourself and all."

"No, not at all, Son." he said. But, if you were buying a blackbird-pie, I'd begin to worry a little. Listen, I gotta get back to work now. Bye bye, Son. See you soon, I hope. Next time bring the girls with you."

***

A month or two later, I was in Dad's store again. I thought it was time to pay him a visit so I went to his office. But his name wasn't on the door this time.

"Where's Ralph?" I asked a team member, "You know, the head of security."

"He's in his office, do you have an

appointment to see him?"

"But this *is* my Dad's office," I said.

"Not anymore. Not since his promotion to store manager. We're all very thrilled to have him heading up our team. He's a great guy and we're all flying high, and morale has never been better since he took over the store. Wait, it looks like he is in, and you said you're his son?"

"That's right. Tell him it's Eric."

Eric enters Ralph's new office

"Wow. Hi Son. Great to see you again. Sit down. What's the occasion, anything special?"

"No, Dad, just shopping for some fish for dinner. I thought I'd drop in and say hello. But I am stunned; what's with the new office and the new title?"

"I guess they told you I'm the store manager now. I goes back to that presentation I was about to make the last time I saw you. Our sales had been a bit flat and if it weren't for the hot dog sales...well I don't know. I recommended a whole new line of pet products to go with our dog and cat food (which by the way is very tasty)...Eric, do you have a cat?"

"No, Dad, no cat. Just a very small dog."

"Good. Anyway, Son, some of the products I recommended are scorching best sellers and our store sales have gone way up, stuff began flying out the doors! The next thing you know, the Regional Office took notice and promoted me to store manager."

"Just what kind of products did you suggest, Dad?"

"Mostly stuff for pets that we didn't carry, a lot of bird stuff, I'm kinda an expert in that department; bird seed in 40 pound packs, electric bird feeders, bird cages with plenty of room to fly....you'd be surprised at the market for bird stuff. But I also recommended some other whiz-bang animal products, Dancing

Duck Welcome Signs for $25, a 24/7 Self Cleaning Cat Litter Box at $350, an elevated outdoor dog bed with sun shade, $64.95, A 'Giant Foo Dog of the Forbidden City Statue, $189, and a best-selling Pet Pressure Washer at $187.

"I gotta tell you, Eric, the other managers snickered when I made my presentation and said my ideas were bird-brained. But the bosses really liked my pitch and I had done my homework with the numbers...the sales forecasts and profit projections.

"So my fellow managers have had to eat a bit of crow, because you can't believe how successful these products have been. Regional Management has been happy as a lark and now all the other stores carry this stuff."

"Fantastic, Dad.   From your human life as a senior marketing executive to a whole new career as a management bird. What a transition. This is the stuff movies are made about."

"Thanks, Son. Say, I hate to cut this short, but the auditors are coming in just a few minutes and I have some stuff to get ready for them."

"I understand, Dad. Love to Leslie."

"Love to your gang too. See you soon, I hope."

***

Well, I hadn't heard from Dad in quite a while and I decided to visit him next time I needed some smoked salmon and batteries. I went into the store and asked to see him.

"Oh, sorry, Ralph's not here anymore," said the team member who recognized me from my last visit. "He just got promoted to the Regional Office. Vice President of Merchandising. We've been the top store in the area for nearly a year now and that didn't go unnoticed by the mucky-mucks at HQ. If you want I can give you his address and phone number."

"Wow. What a surprise! Yes, I'll give him a

call. Thanks."

"Hello, my name is Eric Gullson. Can I speak to Ralph Gullson please. Ok, I'll wait."

On the speakerphone...

"Gullson here. Oh, hi Eric. I've been meaning to call you, sorry about that. This new job just happened in the past couple of weeks, and life has been rather hectic. I guess you visited my store and found me gone."

"Yes, Dad, they said you've been promoted to VP of Merchandising. Wow, this just gets better and better. I guess you've got a fancy office and a big desk and a secretary and all that."

"I do, Son, and lots of people reporting to me. I'm just eating all this up, I feel like I'm in the catbird seat. What a lark! You won't believe this but I'm going to be a speaker at an International Marketing Conference in Boston. Marketing directors from lots of different companies, what an opportunity to meet

people who do what I do—
birds of a feather so to speak."

"Wow, Dad, you can knock me over with a
feath... well you know. I'm really proud of
you. Say when you get back from that
conference will you and Leslie come over for
dinner? Remember, I said we don't have a
cat."

"Sure, Son. I'll have my secretary call you
and set it up. Say, now that I'm an executive
again maybe I can take you under my wing
and help your career?"

"We'll talk about it. Bye, Dad."

The Godmother

Scene: Long Island, New York. A traditional Russian wedding in the large and lavish garden of Nadia and Boris Alekseev -- much dancing and drinking. Orchestra playing fast dance tune. Weather perfect.

The Bridegroom: Sonny Alekseev — a newly minted lawyer. Pa, where's Ma? She should be out here dancing. I gotta go find her.

Boris: Relax, Sonny Boy, your mother is probably in the kitchen topping up the plates of cabbage and raw onion. In spite of all the help we have from the caterers she is wanting always to do everything herself.

Sonny: Well, I'm going to find her. I'm only getting married once, I hope. I want her celebrating with us.

Sonny leaves the garden and walks toward the large colonial house. Before he enters the house he glances through the glass door of the den. He sees a woman in cleaning lady's clothes, kneeling and kissing his mother's hand. Sonny listens through a crack in the open door:

Irena Gorishenko: *a chamber maid at the Palace Hotel in Manhattan.*

So you see, Nadia Chirakov Alekseev, the room supervisors at the hotel daily are stealing my room tips. I need those to live on. It's a terrible situation. One supervisor in particular has been not only stealing, but writing bad reports about my bed making. This Gertrude Ernstbachen, she's an evil person. I think she hates Russians. I'm asking you to use your powers and connections to make justice on that person and stop her from stealing my tips. I'm begging for your help,

Godmother!

Nadia: Irena Kornovia Gorishenko, you come to me to ask a favor on my son's wedding day. Yet you ignore me when I come to collect your monthly union dues. Never a hug, never a Zdravstvuj, or a kiss on the cheek. Never do you call me Godmother. Why do you come to me now?

Irena: I want justice and I know you can do it. Please, Godmother *(kneels and kisses her hand).*

Nadia: All right, because it is my son's wedding day, I will help you. but you will owe me a favor, which I may never collect. Remember that.

Irena: I will. Bless, you Godmother.

Bows and backs up, leaving through the kitchen door. Nadia's "handymen" have been quietly listening from in the back of the room.

Nadia: Ivan, Hugo, get some boys and find out where Gertrude Ernstbachen lives. Don't rough her up, just scare her a little. Let her know her Godmother is watching, and if she steals another tip in that hotel, she'll be soon working as an assistant janitor at the McDonald at the end of the N line in Queens.

Ivan: Okay, GM, we're on it.

The boys leave and Sonny walks into the den.

Nadia: Hi, Sonny Boy, why aren't you out dancing with your bride?

Sonny: Who are these two guys, Ma? And why was that cleaning lady kneeling and kissing your hand?

Nadia: That's Ivan my lawyer and Hugo my CPA. I don't think you've met them before.

Sonny: They look like cheap thugs. And who was that lady?

Nadia: Nah, they're Kharasho, they're okay, and that lady is a client of mine. Listen, Sonnyboychik, you've been away at boarding schools and then college and then law school, we haven't seen much of you in the last few years, and there's a lot you don't know about our family finances. Have you ever thought about how we can live like this, in this big home, on my union organizer's salary? And you can guess your father doesn't make much selling chicken feet.

Sonny: No, Ma, I don't know anything about your finances. I thought maybe you had brought in money from the old country when we came here 18 years ago. I never thought much about it. You and Pa always seemed financially okay.

Nadia: Well, Sonny boy, seeing that it's your wedding day, let me tell you my story.

Nineteen years ago, when you were only six, your father and I got the hell out of Russia. After a year living in Brazil, we were able to come here to the States. What a good break! But our dreams were not so soon realized. We were unable to get good jobs here. In Russia, I was a computer scientist and mathematician, and your father a college professor. The only jobs we could get, maybe because our English wasn't so good at the time, was cleaning lady in an office building for me, and your father, he got a job as a kosher butcher's apprentice. That was before he went off on his own selling chicken feet.

I worked in a big office building down near

the Battery, in the heart of the financial district. I had the 34th floor to clean, and I worked nights for many years and slept days, which Sonnyboychik, is why I didn't see much of you.

One night I was polishing the wood doors to the boardroom in the offices of Horsham Capital. They are investment bankers and venture capitalists, as I later learned, known by their competitors as "Sham Capital." They were famous for company takeovers and then soon selling off assets at a profit, leaving the companies to drift or die. That night, the executives of Sham were having a noisy late-night session. By this time my English was better and I overheard their plan to buy a company whose name I recognized, because it was on the building directory on the main floor of my building. They mentioned the price of this company and I wrote it down. When I got home, I looked it up on the Internet and found that Sham planned to pay $20 a share over the current stock price. So that was news to be dealt with.

We lived in Brighton Beach then, with a lot of other Russians. People called it "Little Odessa". When your father got home from the butcher shop that night, I told him what I had learned and my plan to make some money. We decided, "what could they do to us?" So your father and I contacted all the aunts and uncles and borrowed $20,000, a huge sum for us. I opened an account at a brokerage house, and bought that stock, as much as I could. We didn't make a fortune, but after we paid off the uncles and aunts, we had enough for a nearly-new car. Our first car in this country! There were no Russian cars for sale here, thank goodness, so we bought an American car, a Chevy Nova, blue as I remember. You rode in the back seat. We were in Russian immigrant heaven.

One of our cousins in Brighton Beach, Dmitri Verobev, (I don't think you ever met him), was on the shady side of the law, it was rumored. In fact it was said he was the head of Russian organized crime in New York. Nice man, hard to believe. I asked him if what I had done was illegal. He said: "well maybe to some people," but not as far as he was concerned, and when he learned what I had access to, he wanted in. He told me that he'd heard Sham were a bunch of thieves, and who were we hurting, making money off their shady deals? I could hardly refuse.

Nadia: So I continued to eavesdrop and it got even easier. Dmitri had his people plant microphones in the board room. I could sit and listen in and eat my late night snack of Blinis filled with Tvorog and a side of pickled mushrooms, at the same time.

We began to make piles of money, your father and I. We had to be very careful it didn't show. Eventually we bought this house, a larger car and had enough money to send you to that fancy private day school, and then college and law school.

Sonny: Oh, my goodness! Then what happened?

Nadia: In order to become legit, we set your father up in the chicken feet business and now he controls all the chicken feet sales from Chinatown to Spanish Harlem. I stayed on as a cleaning lady for awhile. It turns out my bosses at the company who had the cleaning contract for the building, had been for years walking all over us cleaning ladies with Cossack boots. Having made a pile of money on tips from Sham, I decided to quit scrubbing floors and become a union organizer.

And I did. I organized a new union for the scrubbers and cleaners in our building and then I began to sign up workers in nearby buildings. Word got out, and soon I had organized over half of the financial district in New York. The big unions tried to muscle in, but I got good protection from Dmitri's people, for which I paid them well, of course. Maybe some kneecaps were broken, I didn't want to know. So they left us alone from then on.

So Sonny Boy, I became looked upon as the savior of the cleaning ladies and they began to call me "Godmother," which in all due modesty, I took as a great compliment. So, I decide to become the Godmother and take care of these poor, wretched cleaning ladies. And what was the harm if I made a few Kopeks doing it? They are lovely people, these ladies, and I still identify with them. We're now totally organized in the financial part of town and we're planning on organizing all the cleaning ladies in all the office buildings and hotels in New York City!

So now, my ladies make a good wage, have medical plans, training programs and child care, all paid for by the miserable capitalist building landlords who rent to terrible companies like Sham. Do I worry about protecting the organization I built? Not so much. You see, I now have judge friends, cop friends, and senator friends. Nobody shakes me down although they've tried. And my lawyers negotiate good contracts with the building owners. They pay up or else their whole place of business will be filthy. When we occasionally go on strike, there's nothing but dirty offices, wharf rats running loose, (ours of course), trash everywhere, dirty windows, ashtrays full, paper cups on floors. Better for them that they pay up. And they do. Now that you're a real lawyer, Sonny, I want you to come into the family business.

Sonny having heard more than he ever wanted to, is speechless. Lively music is heard from the garden.

Nadia: Now, it's your wedding day, let's go out and drink vodka and dance the Kasatski! I see your father out there waving chicken feet and making an ass of himself.

Happy Occasions

The Rules of Engagement

Hello, I'm Wendel. Wendell Whiteside. I have to tell you at the outset, I'm a dog--a Chocolate Labrador Retriever. Actually, I'm Connie Whiteside's dog. Connie's going to be married soon to her boyfriend, Irving Raskin. I don't know if I'm going to live with them after they get married because I gather they'll live in an apartment. Connie hasn't told me yet. If not, I'll be disappointed, of course, but then again, the Whiteside house is really quite palatial, compared to other houses I've been taken to. And I've got a great yard. And Connie's parents, Jack and Christine Whiteside, are goodhearted, really, although when Connie's not around they don't walk me near as much as I'd like.

But enough about me. Connie's engagement dinner was last night. I was there, and it was quite something. Her fiancé's family and our family hadn't met before. It was a near disaster, but it ended okay. If you're interested, I can tell you about it. It's quite an amusing story. Stick around.

Let me start with her fiancé, Irving. Irving's a terrific guy, he always scratches me behind the ears when he comes over here, and has never told me to stop jumping on him (a bad habit of mine which I am trying to break, really). I'm pretty sure Irving is in the footwear business. I think he manages a shoe store. I personally like shoes, most of them are quite tasty, but that's another story. I gather Irving makes an okay living, but it's my mistress, Connie, who has a really good job. She's an Ophthalmologist, an eye surgeon, and she makes a bundle. But it's hard work and she's on her feet all day. Last year she met Irving when she went in to his store to try on some orthotic shoes. And as I said, he's quite a nice guy, and they got to talking and, well, to make a long story short, a year later, there we were at their engagement dinner.

Just a month ago, Connie decide to have a small

dinner party to introduce the two families and to formally announce their engagement. Irving wasn't too keen on this, as I gathered from their conversation, but in the end he gave in. He wrote out a small guest list and she agreed to keep her side of the family down to a few, too. I saw the list, after Connie dropped it accidently, and of course I immediately picked it up and brought it back to her, but not before I'd read it.

Connie and Irving are young and liberal. I wish they were actual tree-huggers, but you can't have everything. I like trees. Connie gets her progressive ideas from her mom and dad who are liberal too, even though they are quite well off. On the other hand, Irving told Connie that his family, despite the fact that they're blue collar, are pretty darn conservative. And, I gather, Irving's mom Ida is not big fan of Connie – not good enough for her son, I suppose. Jack Raskin, Irving's dad is a retired transportation worker (read bus driver) who is the chairman of his local Republican Club. The Raskins are bringing Irving's Aunt Ethel and Uncle Maury Posner. I gather they are very conservativem too (although maybe they were *talking about the Synagogue they go to. I might have this mixed up).*

I do know all about Connie's mom and dad, Doug and Christine Whiteside. They're old money. Doug's a lawyer. He is head counsel for a very important labor union. Doug and Christine support a lot of liberal causes. Christine volunteers at the Museum of Modern Art. She's on the board of several very progressive organizations. The Whitesides belong to a fancy country club (I've never actually been there) and they have a summer house in the Hamptons. They've met Irving a number of times and they like him a lot. Connie has also invited her uncle and aunt, Doug's brother, Roger, who is a Minister, and his wife Julie, a stock broker.

I was having a wonderful nap by the door when the bell rang and the guests began to arrive. Here's what I overheard:

"Ida, just look at this house, the Whitesides must be very rich. And look at this peace sign over the door! Irving said they were liberals but they seem to have so much money I can't see why. And I sure don't see a mezuzah on the door either. We should have brought them one."

"I don't think they're Jewish. Listen Jack, lay off the political stuff for one evening. We don't want to make trouble with our new in-laws."

"Welcome Mr. and Mrs. Raskin. Can we call you Jack and Ida? I'm Christine and this is Connie's father, Doug. Welcome to our home. Come in. And you must be the Posners? Welcome to you too. Our home is your home. Let me take your coats. This is Connie's dog, Wendell, he's very friendly."

I sniffed the Raskins very carefully as they came into the house and I watched them as they checked out the entry way and the living room. They seemed quite surprised at what they saw — beautiful artwork and antiques.

"Wow, this is sure a big house," said Jack. "Doug, what did you say you do for a living?"

"I'm a lawyer, Jack, follow me to the den and let me introduce you to my brother and his wife and we'll have a drink."

Naturally I followed along, dogging their footsteps if you will. I wanted to make certain they didn't take anything. That's the watchdog part in me, I suppose. So we went into the family room where Doug and Connie's sister and brother were waiting. I heard Ida whispering to her husband about the rugs and artwork.

"Wow is that a real Picasso?" she said out of the corner of her mouth, looking at a painting. "Jack, do you think it's real? I wonder how much it cost?"

"Ida, give me a break." he whispered. "These people are loaded. They may be liberal but they're the one percent our party is trying to protect. God love them."

"Doug, why don't you pour everyone a glass of Chardonnay?" said Christine. "Connie and Irving will be here in about half and hour and join us for dinner."

From my advantageous spot under the coffee table I watched Doug introduce Jack and Ida and the Posners to his brother, the Reverend Dr. Ed

Whitesidem and his wife Julie. I overheard Jack make a joke about "tree-hugging Chardonnay drinkers" and then he asked Jack for a whiskey. I don't much care for Chardonnay, either. Gives me gas. Doug and Christine went to the kitchen for the whiskey and some snacks and I followed.

"Chris," said Doug, "I'm sensing these people might be a bit on the right wing side of politics. How did Connie get mixed up with this bunch?"

"Not, Irving, he's okay, he's liberal like us. Hard to believe a working class family like the Posners could be so politically retarded. Let's be careful what we talk about. don't want to alienate our future in-laws."

I followed Doug and the drinks back into the den where I took a strategic positions so I could see and hear everyone. All I heard was polite chatter, as they had their drinks and appetizers. Then Christine announced that dinner would be ready in five minutes.

"So, Christine," said Ida, "you must have a

cook."

"No Ida, I do all the cooking around here. We eat mostly veggie. But I hear that you are a really great cook."

"Who told you that? Irving? He is such a finicky eater. And your daughter Connie, she doesn't eat much either, she could use a couple of more pounds on her."

We all went into the dining room. Connie and Irving entered and joined us. The dinner was buffet style. I really like a buffet. When people help themselves there's always a good chance a bite or two will drop on the floor for me. I was right, Jack dropped a piece of veal and I was right on it. I beat him to it, never mind his nasty glance. They all sat down and Doug made a toast to the engagement of Connie and Irving. Then Ida made a toast:

"So when I heard my son is engaged to a shicksa, I said, 'well my life is over.' But after meeting Bonnie and her family, I don't think it will be quite that bad."

"It's Connie, Mom," said Irving.

"Of course is it. Connie, dear, welcome to the family."

It was all down hill from there. At dinner, the Whitesides talked about slowing down Global warning, and Jack's brother, the minister, talked about the need for Gun Control. Jack's face became a bit red, but he bit his lip said nothing. When it was his turn, he talked about privatizing Social Security, reducing the welfare rolls, and lifting restrictions on oil drilling. The Whitesides and even the Posners just rolled their eyes. Then there was a prolonged silence. You could hear a roll drop, which is what I'd been hoping for. After dessert and coffee, the Raskins announced they had to leave early and headed toward the front door. I followed.

"Thanks for the wonderful evening and dinner, Doug and Christine," said Ida. We have to drop the Posner's off, go home, and watch Fox News, and Jack doesn't like to drive at night."

"We understand dear, thank you so much for coming and for being Irving's parents. I know we'll have many more evenings like this," said Christine, biting her lip. And I'm sure you're going to have a great time at the wedding. Doug's building the kids a chuppa that comes apart, and we can take it to the country club!"

"Oh, the wedding, yes, Well I can bake cookies, and make some casseroles, just let me know. You know those caterers charge an arm and a leg."

"Ida, quick, let's get out of here," said Jack, tugging on her coat.

Jack and Ida and the Posners left in a hurry. I'm glad my tail was away from the door. I thought that was kind of rude. But, anyway, we made it through the evening with no major disasters. After they'd gone, Doug and Christine and Connie and Irving shared another bottle of Chardonnay, and just sat and looked at one another. It was some evening!

I can't wait to go to the wedding and the reception, that's really going to be something, I hope it doesn't turn into a dog fight but I'll be in their corner if they need me. It'll be at the country club and Connie is going to get me one of those service-dog sweaters so they'll let me in. I hope so. I love weddings. I can sing pretty good you know. I hope they ask me.

Dinner at Momma's

Cast of Characters

***Doris, a.k.a. Momma*:** Doris is head of the family now as her husband Morris has retired in more ways than one. She loves to cook and feed people. She's been planning this evening's dinner for two weeks (even though the dishes are the same ones she's been serving for the last 25 years). Doris is an excellent cook and everybody looks forward to a dinner at Momma's.

Morris: Long suffering husband of Doris. Morris is a very nice man and knows it's best if he does what he's told.

Anne and Arnold Cohen: Good friends of Doris and Morris. They don't eat meat and Doris knows it.

Marshall and Aldeane Rifkin: Second

Phil Braverman

cousins to Doris and Morris. They own and run a Kosher butcher shop and they eat a lot of meat. They've been married a long time and often finish each others sentences.

Iz and Bertha Feldman: Iz is a first cousin to Doris. Iz is quite hard of hearing and a little forgetful these days. Bertha is really allergic to cats and dreads visiting her cousin because Doris has a big, black, long haired-cat named Moishe.

Aunt Fanny: Aunt Fanny is a nice lady but kind of dingy. She likes to sing and hum, even at dinner. Her husband is Uncle Mike.

Uncle Mike: Uncle Mike writes poetry that makes no sense at all. He often recites his verse even if not asked. He has a bad habit of telling off-color jokes which he thinks are funny but are often offensive.

Sophie. Sophie is Doris's niece who is in her late 20's and proudly gay--the idea of which the family is finally getting used to. Sophie is well-built and very good looking. This evening she has brought along her girlfriend,

168

Candy, who is about her age and Chinese.

Mona: Mona is Doris's unmarried daughter, Sophie's age. She's brought her fiancé Ralph, who is a Tea Party member and sometime outspoken in his political beliefs, which doesn't sit too well in this family. Mona is on the heavy side and trying to lose about 20 pounds before the wedding, which is planned for four months out.

Doris and Morris are getting ready to greet their dinner guests. Wonderful smells abound.

Doorbell rings

Doris: *from the kitchen* Get the door, bell Morris!

Morris welcomes two couples who arrive at the same time, the Cohens and the Rifkins.

Doorbell

Morris lets in cousin Iz and his wife Bertha.

Morris: COUSIN IZ, YOU CAN PUT YOUR COATS ON THE BED IN OUR BEDROOM!

Iz: Don't shout at me, Morris, I've been here before, you know.

Doorbell rings again

Doris's Aunt Fanny and Uncle Mike enter

Doorbell

Enter Doris's niece Sophie, her girlfriend Candy, and Mona and her fiancé, Ralph.

Doris emerges from the kitchen — her apron still on — smiling, she welcomes everybody:

Doris: Thank you all for coming, it's been awhile since we had a nice quiet family dinner. I hope the people who caused the disturbance last time, and you know who you are, will mind your manners tonight so everybody can enjoy.

Sophie: Are you talking about me? Because if you are talking about me, I'll just leave right now.

Ralph: I think she's talking about me, Soph. *(bunch of Obama-lovers, he mutters to himself)*

Doris: Sophie, dear, we're very glad you are here with your *"friend,"* Candy. Don't get so defensive, we're all friends and relatives. Ralph, you too. You're almost family now.

Now, first a cocktail in the living room. Morris will fix it, and there are some appetizers. I made stuffed eggs and there's salmon on crackers and chopped liver too. Please enjoy and I'll go finish dinner. Everybody's here and we will eat at seven o'clock. Poldark is on PBS at 9:30 and I don't want to miss my program.

Doris leaves for the kitchen. The group moves into the living room where they attack the liver, salmon and stuffed eggs. Morris, unsure as a bartender, pours drinks, and makes them way too strong as usual.

Doris: Dinner is served, good people. We have fruit cup, beef barley soup, brisket with potatoes, kugel, and peas and carrots. I'm saving the dessert as a surprise.

Anne Cohen: Doris, I thought you said you

wouldn't be serving meat tonight. No fish?

Doris: Just a little meat, you need your protein.

Anne: I get all I want without killing animals.

Marshall Rifkin: *(the butcher)* What's that about killing animals? They were raised to feed us. Isn't that right Aldeane? *(she nods in agreement)*.

Anne Cohen: Animals have feelings.

Marshall: Not by the time I get them at my butcher shop. I never heard one complaint from a side of kosher beef! Have you ever heard a side of beef complain, Aldeane?

Anne Cohen: Marshall, you are impossible. Doris, just in case, I brought some veggie-burgers for me and Arnold. Can you warm them for me, Dear?

Doris: Sorry, I thought by now you'd given up that fetish. Of course I'll heat your "veggie burgers." *What a nerve bringing food to my house,* she thought.

Everyone is seated. First course, grapefruit sections and avocado slices.

Doris: Before we eat, I'd like to have a toast. Morris, where is the wine?

Morris: I forgot to put out the wine. Give me a second.

Morris goes downstairs to look for some wine. Moishe the cat takes the opportunity to slink between Morris' feet. He bounds up the stairs and heads straight for the bedroom where the guests coats are piled on the bed.

Doris: While that schmendrick is looking for wine, let's have a toast anyway.   *Uses her water glass.*

Doris: Let's drink to our future son-in-law and our daughter. Even though Ralph votes Republican, we should still welcome him into the family. *(This grates on a couple of people but they keep still about it).* Now let's all eat.

Doris: So tell me Mona, how are the plans for

the wedding?

Mona: We're writing our own service Momma, and the Rabbi is not too happy about that. You know how they love to talk and talk.

Morris: Is that legal what you're doing?

Doris: Young people these days do what they want. Men marry men, women marry women. We are just lucky Mona found a man and we don't have to worry.

Sophie: *(furious)* What did you just say Doris? What if I tell you Candy and I are going to get married!

Doris: That's all right dear. We'll come to the wedding anyway.

Second course: Beef and barley soup

Anne: Don't give me any, please. Arnold, you can eat the soup if you want, it's got beef in it.

Uncle Mike: Where's the beef? *He laughs and recites,* I never saw a purple cow. I never hope to see one. But I can tell you anyhow. I'd rather see than be one.

Mona: That's funny, Uncle Mike.

Iz: Mike, I didn't hear a word you said, could you repeat it, please?

Bertha: Don't encourage him, Iz. He'll just keep it up all through dinner. Iz, have you got your hearing aid on? Please turn it on.

Main course arrives: Brisket with kugel, mashed potatoes and gravy, peas and carrots--plates are filled from the kitchen and served by Grace, who was hired for the evening to help Doris serve and clear, and do the washing up. Plates are brimming full of food--right to the edges. All begin to eat.

Aunt Fanny: Mmm, the brisket is delicious, Doris, although I think there is too much salt in the kugel.

Uncle Mike: Too much salt. Hah, that a good

one. A handshake too many, me thinks!

Doris: *(upset)* I tasted it, it was fine. I saw you put more salt on it before you even tasted it!

Fanny: I did not! I just put on some pepper.

Doris: Listen up everybody! There's more of everything in the kitchen!

Meanwhile, down at the other end of the table…

Sophie: Mona, will you please tell your fiancé to stop staring at my boobs!

Mona: Ralph was not looking at your boobs. What the hell is the matter with you, Sophie?

Sophie: Yes, he was. He bent so far over in my direction he dragged his tie in the soup. Look for yourself. *(Mona looks at his tie, sure enough there is a soup spot)*

Uncle Mike: Sophie, what does a 75 year old woman have between her breasts that a 25 year old doesn't? Her navel. Hah!

Sophie: Uncle Mike, that's disgusting *(others snicker).*

Uncle Mike: Candy, you're Chinese. Do you know these sayings:

Squirrel who runs up woman's leg will not find nuts.

Passionate kiss, like spider web, leads to undoing of fly.

Candy: Uh, well, no, I never heard those.

Sophie: Don't talk to him anymore, Candy, he's a dirty old man. One more like that and we're leaving.

Doris tries to start a civil conversation

Doris: What are we going to do about the homeless in this country?

Ralph: Let 'em get jobs. When they get jobs, they'll find housing.

Mona: That's not nice. If they could get jobs they wouldn't be homeless. What's with you, anyway?

Uncle Mike: A homeless man comes up to me and says: "I haven't tasted food in 3 days."

Don't worry, I told him, it still tastes the same.

Aunt Fanny: I just can't stop him. He thinks everything is a joke.

Iz: Bertha, is Mike asking us for money for the homeless?

Bertha: Did you put batteries in your hearing aid?

Nothing much comes of this discussion. Doris tries to change the topic to the Arab/Israeli peace process with equally disastrous results.

Dessert comes: sherbet and pineapple upside down cake. Coffee and tea are served along with a plate of chocolates.

The men go into the living room--stuffed--taking their coffee along. Uncle Mike loosens his pants and lays down on the floor. Morris turns on the TV to the sports channel. There is a boxing match going on. Everybody is talking and shushing. Cousin Iz is passed out in an armchair--he passes gas about every 5 minutes like Old Faithful.

Ralph and Marshall get in a big argument about Obamacare. There is a knockout on the TV and the room quiets for a moment. Morris gets up and changes the channel to the nine o'clock news.

The ladies are in the kitchen, putting things away. "Take some food home," Doris tells them, and shovels leftovers into containers she had spread out on the counter.

Morris: Doris *(he shouts)*, your program is almost on!

The guests begin to leave. Bertha goes upstairs and finds black cat hair all over her favorite white coat. She is furious. She can't put it on for fear of having an asthma attack. Moishe the cat, whose sleep was rudely disturbed, is now hiding under the bed. The guests, their coats on, (except Bertha) all leave.

Doris: *(standing at the front door):* Thanks for coming everyone, I hope you all had enough to eat.

Aunt Fanny: Thanks for a wonderful party, Doris.

Bertha: *(mumbling to herself on the way to the*

car) God damn cat. I'll never come here again. And the kugel *was* too salty.

Iz: Bertha, were we at the right house? I didn't recognize any of those people.

Here Comes the Bride

Wedding Bells!

Dr. Jill Furtner and Andrew Blandstein were married on January 22nd at the Pool restaurant in the Seagram building in New York. Rabbi Rachael (formally Richard) Rubinstein officiated. The bride's three year old son Compton, was the ring barer. The best man was Irving Waxon, Mr Blandstein's best friend and former parole officer. The maid of honor was the bride's first cousin, Assemblywoman Sylvie Gomper, Democrat 12th assembly district. Rabbi Rubinstein, it should be noted, is the Cities' first black, transgender, Catholic convert to be ordained a rabbi.

Dr. Furtner, 38, is a Neurosurgeon at Mt Zion Hospital and a member of the Bronx Borough Council. She is on the board of the

Whitney Museum, the Women's Board of the Met, and is on the board of the Lung Cancer Research Foundation in New York City.

She is the daughter of Ramon Furtner of New York and Miriam Furtner of Atlantic City. The bride's father is the head of the Law firm of Furtner, Lewis and Hopstein, and vice president of the global banking firm of Dewey-Furtner and Company. He is also a backer of many Broadway shows including Hamilton, Hello Dolly, and Carousel, which is now on tour, and previews in Boston in March. Mr. Furtner attended Columbia on a rowing scholarship, and Harvard Law school where he was president of the Law Review.

The bride is also the step-daughter of Furtner's current wife Nicole Ratner-Furtner who is on the board at the Lincoln Center and heads up the annual Black and White Gala this year.

The bride's mother, Miriam Furtner, lives in Galveston, Texas, and works as a cocktail waitress on an oil rig. Due to bad weather in the channel she was unable to attend the wedding.

The bride's previous two marriages ended in divorce.

Mr. Blandstein, 41, is currently a personal trainer and male escort. Formerly. he was head of Pediatric surgery at New Jersey General until he was terminated for not having a medical degree. Mr. Blandstein attended Yeshiva University for four years but was not actually enrolled.

The groom's first marriage ended in the unsolved disappearance of his wife, Florence. There were no children.

Mr. Blandstein is the son of Milton and Reva Blandstein of Del Vista Primo - Unit B, in Boca Raton, Florida. The senior Mr. Blandstein is a retired Tallis salesman. Previously he owned a fountain pen repair shop. Before her retirement, the groom's mother, Reva, was a quality control technician for Alpo pet foods.

The bride and groom met at a performance of Hamilton where the groom volunteered in the coat check room. It was love at first sight after she saw him wearing her fur coat at intermission. They had their first date at the Bronx Zoo where they fed the chimps and briefly attended the sea lion show.

The bride will change her name from Dr. Jill Furtner to Dr. Denise Furtner-Blandstein

The couple will honeymoon in Acapulco where the Mr. Blandstein still has cartel connections.

After the honeymoon, the couple will be living in Dr. Furtner's apartment in the City.

Family Secrets

The Fake Job - Employment Agency

"Hello this is the FJEA, Camille Sanson speaking. How can I help you?"

"Hi, my name is Bruce Farquhar. I'm the CEO of Magnolia Moldings, Inc. I need to hire someone for a position that we really ought to eliminate. I hear you have people who don't work too hard and won't make waves."

"We sure do, Mr. Farquhar. Can you tell me about the job opening."

"We'll, you see, it's to fill a position of a person who just retired after 40 years. We have no idea what she was doing, so we don't need much in the way of skills. Just someone who will show up most of the time."

"Yes, yes, Mr. Farquhar, we have a lot of people who would qualify for that. Very little skill or talent, but they would show up, especially if they had a nice desk. And coffee, and maybe long lunch hour.

"Tell me, what does Magnolia Moldings do?"

"We do moldings. Industrial moldings."

"Is that molding like you see on the ceilings of a house, or castings, like when you make a statue. or false teeth?"

"Yes, yes, I think it is. Can you send me some resumes?"

"Yes, of course, how much does the job pay?"

"I'm under the impression the person who retired was getting $40,000. No one seems to know exactly. Is that enough? There are fringe benefits of course, health insurance, vacations, etc. "

"Yes, I think we can find you someone well qualified to do what you're looking for. Are you looking for someone with special talents or experience?"

"Nah, we're just looking to hire someone who won't do anything or break anything or upset anybody — our employees, and especially our customers."

"Sounds good. I'll send you the resumes of two of three of our clients who have never broken anything, then you let me know who you want to interview."

"That would be great."

"Thanks so much for calling FJEA."

Hangs up

Calling…

"Hello, Harold, I think we have just the right

job for you. I sent them your resume and they are very interested."

"What doing, Aunt Camille?"

"Nothing—just showing up"

"Show up **every** day?"

"Let me check with them and get back to you on that. It's a great opportunity"

"What do you mean opportunity? You know I have no aspirations."

"Well you did answer the phone just now."

"Yes, well I happened to be standing next to it. I didn't have to get out of my chair—I was already out."

"Out of your chair, well that counts for something. Listen, do you think you could make it to an interview if I set one up for you?"

"I don't know. Will they send a car?"

"It's possible. I think they might."

"Okay. Well then, why not."

"Do you want to know what the job pays?"

"Not especially. No."

"Goodbye, Harold. I'll call to give you the interview date. And please answer your phone. And let me know how the interview went."

Honestly, I don't know why I bother with Harold. I have a whole drawer full of people who have inherited money, won the lottery, have rich fathers, ex congressmen, and judges. Well, it is my sister's kid.

At the job interview

"Hi, Mr. Farquhar, I'm Harold Garberfeld. the Agency sent me over. Am I late?"

"Just half and hour, but that's ok, Harold. Glad you showed up at all. Now that you're here sit down and let's talk. Tell me about yourself."

"Okay. Well after college I waited around

for a good job to come along."

"Did you go out and try to find one?"

"No. Are you supposed to do that?"

"Well, I don't really know. My father brought me into this business."

"Can you tell me about the job?"

"Yes. Well the person in the job just retired. We're not quite sure what she did so there is plenty of room to do whatever you want."

"What would that be?"

"You know, make decisions about moldings, fine tune the job, that sort of thing."

"I guess I could do that. Can I ask you about money and benefits?"

"Sure, what about them?"

"Well, what are they?"

"Oh. Listen, Personnel will fill you in on the detail. I think the job pays $40,000 a year but it could be more. Will that work for you?"

"I guess for now, when could I start? I have a three week cruise I'd like to take and then there is my cousin's graduation in Atlanta, and then....I guess I could start in about six weeks. Is that okay?"

"Listen, Harold with your qualifications, we'll be happy to see you whenever you show up."

"Gee thanks, Mr. Farquhar. You probably won't regret hiring me."

"Just call me Bruce, son"

"Thanks, Bruce, dad."

Six months later...

"Hi, Harold, it's Aunt Camille. Since you haven't called me, I'm calling to follow-up on you. Mr. Farquhar said he made you an offer and he's paid our finders fee. So I guess he hired you. How are you doing?"

"Oh, hi, Aunt Camille. I've been meaning to call. Yes, yes, I did get hired. I've been real busy at work thinking about new uses for moldings."

"Is the job okay? Are they treating you nicely?"

"Oh yes, Dad, I mean, Bruce, I mean Mr. Farquhar, seems to like me. I already got a raise and a promotion and a nicer desk. I think he's grooming me to take over the company when he retires."

"And when might that be?"

"Couple of months, I think. Soon as he clears it with the Board. By the way, I am on the Board of Directors now."

"How nice for you."

"I don't know, it's a lot of responsibility. And all those moldings. What are you going to do?"

"Keep in touch, Harold. Let me know if you need to hire someone to take over your old job. Your cousin Carol is available, her mother tells me."

The Return of the Mail Order Bride

My Cousin, Murray Kahn, PhD, professor of Chinese history at UC Berkeley, couldn't get a date to save his life. He tried Jdate, Match.com, and (his mother shouldn't know), Christian Mingle. Oh, he got leads all right, but they were all losers in his opinion. He was looking for an intellectual and spiritual soul mate, attractive with good social skills, a great cook and an interesting conversationalist. Results to-date were predictably low.

One day, while doing research on 20th Century Zigong history and perusing microfilm of newspapers of that period, he came upon an advertisement for Chinese Brides available for shipment to the United States. The ad had photographs of beautiful women and explained that all their brides had been checked out for social skills, cooking, and conversation. Being a history professor, he remembered that this practice stopped just after 1920 but many thousands of *picture brides* had legally entered the U.S. and its territories.

Murray did a little research on the Internet and found that *picture brides* from Asia are still available. But it's now a matchmaking service, not a wife-in-the mail, as in the 20's. Just for fun, and to exercise his skills in the Chinese language, he decided to write to the nearly 100 year-old address he copied from the 1918 newspaper. He thought, if anyone answered, he could learn more about the history of those so-called mail order brides.

In a couple of weeks he received a letter (in English) from a Nathan Chong, explaining that the original matchmaking service belonged to his great grandfather, who was long gone, but it was still possible to get a picture bride from China, as a lot of young Asian women would like to come to America. Further, the rates for such a hookup were very reasonable. Would he (Murray), like some more pictures? Several pictures were sent with Nathan's letter whose letterhead read:

New Lucky Brides.

Excited about a new source of possible companionship, Murray decided to pursue the matter. He screened a number of resumes that Nathan sent by email, and one in particular caught his eye: a Miss Sarah Oolong. It began with her vital statistics:

Age: 25

Hair: *Black, what else*

Weight: *50 kilos*

Height: *5'1"*

Build: *Average or better*

Education: *Masters degree in English Literature*

Occupation: Import/Export

Languages: Mandarin, English, French

Likes: *Conversation, classical music, literature, and cooking (Asian and French)*

Sarah Oolong went on to describe what an intelligent and loving person she was, and that she was looking for a suitable "Prince Charming," looks and age not all that important.

With hopes high, Murray picked up the phone, dialed long distance and in his best Mandarin, began to discuss the transaction with Nathan Chong, the owner of New Lucky Brides. Nathan assured him of complete satisfaction or his money back. After all, New Lucky Brides had a reputation to uphold.

Soon after, he paid a fee (credit card okay) and he was able to begin contact with Sarah Oolong. They communicated on the Internet by instant message:

"Hello, Sarah, I'm Professor Murray Kahn."

"Hi. Professor Murray. Did you know Kahn is a very popular Chinese name. Do you have any Chinese relatives?"

"I think way back when some relatives escaped Russia and came to the States by way of Shanghai, a cousin or two might have stayed in China. Tell me about yourself, may I call you Sarah?"

And so it went. They corresponded daily for two weeks and Murray was really excited by Sarah and the prospect that he might have found his true love. He offered to fly over to China to meet her, but she insisted that she come to the States.

So Murray sent her a ticket, and a few weeks later, he picked her up at the San Francisco airport. She was as beautiful as her picture, but appeared to be a bit older than advertised. Not a big problem.

After sending Nathan Chong more money, per their agreement, Murray and Sarah began to learn more about each other. It didn't take Murray long to find out that Sarah, smart as she was, was a demanding witch. Nothing was ever good enough for her. All the sweetness she had shown in their instant messages was apparently just for show. (And her sweet and sour chicken dish wasn't all that good either).

Murray made a phone call to Nathan Chong.

"Hello, Nathan. It's Murray. Listen, this thing with Sarah Oolong isn't going to work out. Not at all. I'd like you to talk to her and tell her she has go home, and I'd like my money back for the match, please."

"I'm really sorry, Professor. I'll send you an RMA number, an address label, and an air ticket. You can ship her back to me when you get the paperwork."

Murray waited for the airline ticket and the paperwork. Meanwhile Sarah Oolong made his life miserable, just about every waking moment. He'd be so happy when she was on the plane back to China.

Two weeks later a telegram arrived. It was from Nathan.

Unable to process your return. Stop. But we have sent a replacement. Stop. She arrives tomorrow at SFO, name: Margaret Oolong. Stop.

Murray got right on the phone: "What the hell are you doing to me, Nathan! I didn't want a replacement, I wanted to start all over, or maybe not at all."

"Sorry, Professor," said Nathan, "I thought you'd be pleased...and just to show our goodwill you can keep Sarah Oolong too."

"Oh, my God, another Oolong! I'll bet this is her sister, right?"

"Let me check," said Nathan. "Yes, it is, her younger sister. I think you'll like her."

Sarah and Murray headed for the airport and met Margaret Oolong at passenger arrivals. The ladies jabbered away in Mandarin all the way home to Berkeley. It was a swell reunion for them, and at least Murray didn't have to pay the airfare this time.

Murray decided to give Nathan Chong one more chance to fix this mess. He sent an Email demanding that Nathan take these ladies back, or else. He just couldn't handle them. Nathan replied that he was on it, and that there was a good solution, and that Murray should be patient.

Days passed, and as Murray was leaving for class one morning, a cab pulled up and an Asian lady got out. Sarah and Margaret ran to her and began to jabber so fast in Mandarin that Murray could only guess that this was Rose Oolong, their mother.

"I sent her to keep the other ladies in order while we are working on the return issues," said Nathan, responding to Murray's frantic phone call.

The days went by, Murray kept busy at his teaching job. The ladies were happy to be with each other all day, and somehow kept busy too. It turns out that Rose Oolong was a fantastic cook, and the big old house Murray's parents left him had never been so tidy. Rose Oolong said that she had been in the restaurant business in China and was thinking of opening a place here in Berkeley. Why not, thought Murray, she's a great cook and her daughters can work there too: it'll get them out of my house.

So with financial help from Murray, Rose opened The Happy Harbor House, specializing in Zigong dishes. Reviews were terrific and word got out, and soon people were lined up on the sidewalk waiting to eat there.

Seizing the moment, Rose (with Murray's backing), opened a second location and that, too, did exceptionally well. By now Murray was pretty used to having the ladies there and they were all so busy they hardly ever collided. He'd never eaten better, or lived in a cleaner house.

One day another Asian young lady showed up at the door with her suitcase. It was Rose's niece, Sylvia Oolong.

"Murray, our businesses are booming and I needed an accountant to keep track of the books." said Rose, "So here she is. My niece Sylvia has an MBA and the Zigong equivalent of a CPA. Sylvia, I'd like you to meet our good friend and business partner, and your landlord, Murray Kahn."

Murray began to talk to her in Mandarin, but she preferred to answer in perfect English

"I'm really looking forward to being with all of you, especially you, Murray," said Sylvia, "I'm very interested in Chinese history and I am sure I can learn a lot from you and maybe teach you a few things, too."

Murray was dazzled and instantly smitten. Sylvia was a knockout. Drop dead gorgeous. A CPA too!

"And by the way," said Sylvia, "I bring you warm regards from our cousin, Nathan Chong. He said he's still trying to process your return – he said you'd know what that meant."

"I do know, but I think we're good now."

Outsourcing Grandma Sylvia

"Senior care homes on the rise in India. Traditional family life now shifting."

Sacramento Bee, Sunday, May 20th, 2012

"What are we gonna do about mom?" I asked my wife Judy. "Dad didn't leave her much, and nice as it is to have her with us, she's been moping around the house lately looking sad-faced--even the dog avoids her. I wish we could find her a great place that's affordable and safe, where she can get wonderful food, live in beautiful surroundings, and get loving care."

A few weeks later I was waiting for a haircut and reading one of those magazines for senior citizens, from AARP or something. I came across this ad:

Save 40--60%. No money down, no buy-in,

affordable, safe, loving care, wonderful food, and beautiful surroundings. Reply to 1-888-555-7732 or visit our website: www.saveonseniors.com/in

I replied to the ad, and soon Judy and I attended a sales presentation along with a lot of other folks with ageing parents. We learned about a great place for mom to live at a price we could afford. Turns out that India, always looking for opportunities to score US dollars I guess, built this government-sponsored "Assisted Living Zone" near a beautiful river close to Bangalore. They constructed several retirement communities and assisted living facilities that are carbon copies of the ones you find in Boca Raton, Sun City Phoenix, and the Catskills.

To make them home-like they built a Costco and a Trader Joe's; churches, synagogues, Kaiser Health services, two Charles Schwab offices, a bank of America, a Safeway, and a Food Giant. Their satellite TV has Oprah and all the popular U.S. programs and Radio India plays all the popular talk shows.

We learned that American newspapers are downloaded daily from the Internet, printed and delivered to the residents; all part of the package. Local post offices are there to mail letters and serve as voting precincts.

Our conclusion after hearing the sales pitch was that if we could just get her to go there, Mom would be really happy and might never suspect she was in Bangalore. We'd tell her she was going to live in Sun City, Phoenix! Best of all, at these prices, we could afford to give her the lifestyle she deserves!

***

After the limo picked her up at the airport in Bangalore, Sylvia was whisked away through the crowded, noisy streets. It was late at night and she couldn't see much out of the tinted window. Still groggy from the long flight, she dozed off.

The sun was coming up and Sylvia woke up when the limo stopped. "Welcome to Sun City East," the sign said. She was escorted by her driver into a beautiful lobby and welcomed by a line of uniformed staff. She was ushered straight up to a spacious, well-furnished apartment, where two ceiling fans made a pleasant whirring sound. Isn't it curious, she thought, the staff doesn't look Filipino or Samoan like at the other places my kids showed me. Here they look more Indian or Pakistani. Oh well, I'm sure they are nice and I hope the food is good. The place looks just like the pictures in the Sun City East brochure. I'm very tired from the trip and this wonderful room has a very nice looking bed.

We were so happy when we got our first letter from Mom. It sounded like she was getting along just fine.

Dear Paul and Judy and kids,

I am enjoying my first few days here at Sun City East. It was a little strange getting here. When you put me on the plane in Minneapolis, I thought it would be about a four-hour flight but it sure seemed a lot longer.

It was very dark when I got off the plane, and during the long walk to the baggage area, I saw strange faces and heard the sing-song of a language that I did not understand. But then, this was the Phoenix airport, so what else could you expect?

I miss you a lot but I am really settling in nicely. Everyone is so friendly, and as I was telling Parvati, the lady who cleans my room, I'm really enjoy the food. A vegan diet has been something I've always wanted to try. Oh, and the grounds are just beautiful-- walkways of tile, many fountains, and statues and tropical plants. I've enclosed a picture of a beautiful large bird with amazing plumage

Phil Braverman

that lives in our garden. One of the staff, Kapoor, tells me it's an Arizona Twill bird. I'll write more soon.

Love you all, Mom

***

The hot summer days drifted by, and then the monsoons came. Sylvia fit in well with the other ladies and a few gentlemen; they all seemed happy to be at Sun City East. It was quite hot outside in the garden, but Sylvia guessed that was to be expected in the Phoenix area, especially at that time of year. There were a few Gibbon monkeys swinging through the Peepul trees. A nice fun touch, thought Sylvia. Surprisingly there were few visitors, but Skype was readily available. After some brief training by Ranjit, a nice man on the staff, residents talked with their relatives often, as computers were abundantly available throughout the complex.

On shopping days many of the residents boarded a bus and were transported to a beautiful shopping center with tile fountains and statues of elephants. It did seem a little odd riding through the streets of downtown Phoenix and seeing cows, oxen and elephants. Sylvia thought the circus was surely in town.

They shopped at the Costco, Nordies, Trader Joe's and Safeway. At least that's what the signs said. The stores looked a bit strange inside. Lots of silk scarves next to white linen baggy trousers and tops, with a sign that said *Mundus,* and that was at Nordies. Costco carried the usual stuff but had stacks of Saris in the clothing area, heaps of sandals of all sizes and shapes, and great bags of rice. TJ's strangely had very little meat in the refrigerated cases, but the spice department covered twelve running feet of shelf space!

Back home from shopping, and after a delicious veggie lunch with jasmine tea, it was usually nap time for most residents. Or, TV if you were so inclined. Cable played all the channels the residents were used to and then some. There was a lot of TV coverage of a sport called Cricket. Sylvia was fascinated, and she was beginning to learn how the scoring is done.

Dear Judy and Paul,

I guess it's been two months now since I got to Sun City East. I am really enjoying my stay here. The staff is so cheerful, and funny too. They do talk a bit fast for me though. I had an upset stomach last week and I saw the nicest doctor, Dr. Kashani. He said I had Delhi-belly (I didn't understand that at all) and he gave me some herbal meds — it cleared me up just like that!

Anyway, one of the staff, Ranjit Sitlani is teaching me how to use Skype, so we can see each other in person. I'll soon be able to do just that. I know it's hard for you to get away for a visit, especially this time of year! Give the kids hugs for me. Sorry this note is so short, I am really busy with all the activities here. More later.

Love, Mom.

Some six months into her stay, Sylvia, newly energized by her pleasant surroundings, began to get a bit bored. Not that there wasn't enough to do; she was very active on the Resident's Board of Sun City East and she was elected treasurer by voice vote.

One day a resident handed Sylvia a new book: *The Best Exotic Marigold Hotel*, the story of elderly English tourists at a run-down hotel in India. She read the book in two days and really enjoyed it. Oh my goodness, she thought, after reading a couple of chapters, I'm not in Phoenix, I'm in India! I guess Paul and Judy knew all about this. Oh my! I really do like it here and I'm going to take a page from this book and see if I can find myself a job.

The next afternoon, walking to tea on the veranda, she read a help-wanted sign posted on the bulletin board.

English-Speaking person wanted for customer service work on the telephone. Full-time or part-time. Must have pleasant voice and be able to learn about certain products and services to help customers solve problems. Good pay. Nice working conditions.

Sylvia thought about it over a cup of sweet tea, and a day or two later took some action. She hired on as a call center trainee at the Customer First Call Center. She thought it best not to tell the kids until she saw how it worked out.

Dear Judy and Paul:

Can you believe it, I've been here six whole months now and I just love it. I'm keeping very busy with all the activities here. I'm on the Resident's Board and you'd be proud of me — they elected me Treasurer.

Anyway, keep me in your thoughts and for goodness sakes, don't worry about me.

Love, Mom

***

We hadn't had a letter from Mom for a few weeks and we hadn't Skype'd recently either. I began to get a little concerned. Then one day my cable TV went out. I called the Comcast 800 number to get a fix on when it would be working again. Usually the people at the other end of those phones are very hard to understand but after punching in numbers 6 times to get to talk to a real person, I got connected to a very clear-speaking customer service rep. She asked me about my problem and as we talked, I began to think there was something very familiar about that voice.

"MOM?"

"Mr. Gerstein, I am working on your request, Sir."

"Mom? Mom, is that you?"

"Sir, we are not allowed to have a personal conversation with our customers. But I am pleased to tell you your TV service will be fully restored within 24 hours. And, please give Judy and the kids a hug for me. And, don't worry about me, I am not angry with you, not the least bit. Sun City East is all that it was cracked up to be. I always wanted to visit India, and I'm just lovin' it!"

Birth of a Notion

"He never calls," said Miriam to her husband Henry, who was buried deep in his newspaper.

"What do you mean he never calls, you talked to him last week."

"That was last week, I mean *this* week. What kind of son doesn't call his mother every week?"

"Most sons, I would imagine," said Henry. "I think you expect too much of Melvin. He's a grown man and he's got his own life."

"What life? A life without involving your mother and father? What if he gets sick and we don't find out? What if his wife leaves him?"

"Miriam, he's not married. What are you talking about?"

"I'm going to do something about it. Just

look at this article in the AARP magazine."

Chinese Government Gets It Right For A Change

- *New Chinese law requires children to visit elderly parents*
- *Care of growing elderly population a big challenge for China's leaders*
- *One-child policy and economic reform have broken up extended family*
- *Some say law controversial and hard to enforce*

__Hong Kong (CNN)__ -- Lola Wang, a 28-year-old marketing officer in Shanghai, makes a six-hour trip to Shandong province in eastern China to see her parents twice a year -- once during the Lunar New Year and again during the National Day holiday in October.

"I feel like I should visit my parents more but having a job in the financial industry means I have to work long hours and sacrifice some of my personal time for work," Wang, an only child, tells CNN.

Wang's dilemma is faced by many young people in

China, where a one-child policy and three decades of economic reforms have accelerated the decline of the traditional extended family.

It's also a matter of concern for China's new leaders as they grapple with the burden of supporting the growing number of elderly people.

"So what Miriam. That's China. We don't have laws like that here."

"So maybe it's time we had such a law! Then Melvin would have to call, and I'd know when he got sick or if his wife is leaving him."

"I keep telling you, he's not married, Miriam!"

"I'm going to take this article to my bridge club and see what they think. Then I'm going to send it to all my friends and have them email it to their friends."

At her bridge club, Miriam read out loud the article about the new Chinese law. Her bridge pals were unanimous in their support of the idea. They suggested that Miriam speak at the monthly Senior Center meeting and she agreed. She read the article to that audience; there must have been over a hundred seniors.

The room was hushed, the audience stunned. Then Miriam spoke:

"Fellow mothers, and some fathers too, of our thoughtless, no good sons and daughters, let's unite! You shouldn't let your ungrateful kids walk away from you as you approach your twilight years. You can be just as involved with the details of their lives as when they were young, if you play your cards right. Let's form an organization to protect our rights as parents. Then we can get laws passed so your sons and daughters won't neglect you anymore. It's your right and privilege, so remember that. Now I'm taking signups. So raise your hands."

Wild applause, and almost everyone raised their hands.

And so a new organization was formed, and a group of leaders selected to be on the Board of Directors, headed, of course, by Miriam Greenbelt. They got help from a lawyer, Mrs. Plotkin's son, Arnold, and they formed a non-profit corporation. They named it the *American Society for the Prevention of Cruelty to Parents (ASPCP)*, with the charter of:

- Establishing conduct standards for grown children which outline their duties to their parents; including a reasonable number of telephone calls and visits, suitable birthday gifts, rides to the doctor, meals out, attendance at family events and religious ceremonies.
- Affirming the right as parents to interfere with our children's lives when we think it's the best thing for them.
- Getting Congress to pass a law just like they did in China, only in English.
- Publishing a monthly newsletter with tips for dealing with kids who ignore you.

With a start up grant from the Hallmark Greeting Card Company (after Hallmark received a letter requesting funds from Miriam Greenbelt with the promise of a lot of new birthday and anniversary card business) they rented modest office space, and installed a computer with help from one of the good sons of a Board member. He helped them set up a Facebook page and Twitter account. News about the ASPCP spread quickly among seniors across the country.

The ASPCP began to publish their monthly E-newsletter entitled: **"KIDS: what are you going to do about them?"** They published articles like, *"Using Food as a Weapon of Love."* *"How to be caretaker of your kids forever through endless self-sacrifice."* *"11 Powerful Steps to Guilt Inducement."*

They also published letters to the editor. Here are some letters from loyal readers:

Dear KIDS:

I'd like your good advice for my problem which, of course, is my son. He's only 42 but already he disobeys me. *Especially at the dinner table. He won't finish his grapefruit cocktail, doesn't eat all his meat and potatoes, and never, never asks for seconds, although God knows there is a lot more in the kitchen. He says he's become a vegetarian and I never even knew he was religious.*

So what can I do to get him to eat better? When he won't eat I tell him, "go to your room, " but that really doesn't work well as (and I've just recently learned this) he has his own apartment downtown and doesn't live here anymore. I wonder who's doing his laundry?

I'd like to know what you have to say about this.

Thank you,

Zelda Ricci

New Jersey

Dear Zelda:

Clearly your son has an eating disorder and should be seen by a doctor, preferably with a degree from a good school, very soon.

Editor, KIDS

Dear KIDS:

My problem is my daughter-in-law. She thinks she has priority. My son has to get her permission before he can help his parents with small chores like repainting our kitchen, or taking out a dead tree (where, by the way, he used to have a swing). If she had her way he'd spend all his time with her and his kids (who, by the way, are unmannered little brats and ill-raised, if you ask me).

What can I do to put her in her place and let my son know that his first responsibility is to his parents who raised him to always dress warmly and vote Democratic?

Melba Arnold

California

Dear Melba:

If I were you I'd begin to look for a new wife for him. Clearly this one isn't working out. His loyalties are obviously misdirected and it's her fault, make no mistake. Act quickly while the kids are young and a change can be made without much notice.

Editor, KIDS

Dear KIDS:

My problem is my son. He refuses to meet the girls I have in mind for him. Take Zelda, for example, a college graduate and a real looker. All right so she is a few pounds overweight, but that can be fixed. Or Ruthie, who is a lawyer with a wonderful set of parents with whom I am close. Even though she is a Republican, could you find a better match?

What have you got to say for yourself?

Anonymous (Mrs.)

Florida

Dear Reader:

I know why you are anonymous. And Ma, I've told you many times to stop writing to this column. It won't do you a bit of good. I'm still serious about Alan, my partner of 10 years. We're planning to adopt so you may have a grandchild after all if you play your cards right. Stop feeling guilty, it's not your fault!

Editor, KIDS

So the ASPCP began to grow, and by charging very modest dues they were able to expand their office space and hire staff. Their enthusiastic Board held a planning session generating a lot of good ideas and an action plan which included:

- A massive membership drive. *We'll hire a PR firm and raise buckets of money.*

- Their own PAC. *We'll use our dues and contribution money to form a Political Action Committee, and we'll hire top notch lobbyists to bug congress people about our cause and pass a new law.*

"We'll teach these ungrateful kids they can't neglect us." said Miriam to the group. "How does that sound? Let's hire us a PR firm and find a lobbyist or two and we're off and running."

The ASPCP hired the PR firm, Abner, Dolby and Crisp, the same firm that handles the ASPCA, the animal protection people, who have been very successful at fundraising over the years. They raise nearly $40 for every stray dog in America. No one knows what they do with all that money.

The PR firm created a promotional plan with billboards and TV ads showing pictures of forlorn and mistreated parents, living in horrible conditions, sniffling, and looking so sad you just want to send in your money, or maybe at least take one home. In one picture, a ragged old lady holds a sign:

"Son won't answer my calls. Adoption fee waived...please!"

They hired the hotshot lobbying firm, *P Street*, who began to call on members of Congress to lobby to get elder parent protection legislation on the congressional agenda.

They were met with resistance until they figured out they were talking to the wrong people. So they began a campaign aimed at the parents of the members of Congress, especially the older members. Their campaign slogan was: *If not now, soon it'll be your turn!* They asked the parents of the Senators and House Members to put pressure on their elected sons and daughters. Their message was well received.

"John, this is your mother, Edna."

"I know your name, Ma. What do you want, I'm in a very important meeting. How did you get through to me?"

"Tell me you're going to support a new law

to help us older parents."

"What new, law Ma? Say, who gave you this number?"

"The law you're going to pass, and the sooner the better. By the way, when are you coming for a visit?"

"Mom, the Middle East is on fire and I've got a pipeline to build."

"Jonny, can I help? Can I at least make you sandwiches while you're building the pipeline?"

"Sure, Ma. Listen, the President is waiting, I really gotta go."

The tactic worked and soon the ASPCP lobbyists were met with friendly greetings in the Congressional halls and offices.

Using the Chinese law as a model, the lobbyists crafted a new bill and then began to look for members of Congress to sponsor it. The bill spelled out the rights of older parents and the duties of their children to respect those rights, and provide financial and other support...*without having to be asked all the time!*

"I suggest that Congresspersons who are getting on in years and will soon benefit from our work, might sponsor the bill," said Miriam to Paul Abner, head lobbyist.

"Right on, Mrs. G. There are lots of old farts in Congress who will soon enough be on the streets themselves," said Abner. "They're hoping their kids will be nice to them in their declining years. Five members of Congress are now in their 80's and nineteen are in their 70's. Lets go after them to co-sponsor the bill, it's an easy sell."

Abner was right, and with bipartisan sponsorship from nearly all the senior members, plus continual pressure from congressional mothers, both houses of Congress passed the bill. The President was somewhat reluctant to sign the bill (because it came with a rider to put a new coat of paint on the Alaskan Bridge, to Nowhere) but he folded under pressure after his wife's mother threatened to move in with them.

So with great fanfare and everybody taking credit, Federal Statue 4626, the *Parent Protection Act* was signed into law and the ASPCP began to look for a test case.

"I have an idea who it should be," said Miriam. With the help of their staff attorney, she brought suit against her own son, Melvin Greenbelt, for "serious" violation of the new *Parent Protection Act.*

When Melvin was served a subpoena to appear in court, he was overheard to have muttered, "Oh shit, she's at it again. She'll never let go. Why didn't I run away from home when I had the chance?"

Naturally the news media got wind of all this and Melvin became somewhat of a celebrity. He was cheered on by ungrateful sons everywhere who were very much against the *PPA*, and jeered at by older parents who viewed him as a villain; one to be quickly tried, convicted and punished...and not just to stand in a corner!

Melvin pleaded "not guilty" which made his mother even angrier because she thought that over the years she had been able to make him feel plenty guilty. "I just didn't do my job," she said to her husband. The trial was set for May 12th, Mother's Day that year, and a large courtroom was booked because of all the interest by the media and the public.

As good friends of Miriam, we were lucky enough to get a seat at the trial. Here's what happened to Melvin:

The Trial

Bailiff: Hear Ye, Hear Ye, the Court is now in session. All rise for the Honorable Brighton Brighton.

Brighton: Please be seated, folks. Bailiff, will you read the charges in this case.

Bailiff: Yes, your Honor. In the matter of the People vs. Melvin Greenbelt, the defendant, Mr. Greenbelt, is accused of violating Federal Statute 4626, the *Parent Protection Act*.

Brighton: I see we have Prosecuting Attorney, Dorcas Marcus, for the People. How are you today, Dorcas?

Dorcas: Just fine Judge, thank you.

Brighton: And the attorney for the defendant, Dee Fence. Welcome to my court, Dee.

Members of the Jury, welcome to you. And thank you for serving.

Brighton: Will the attorney for the People please enlighten the court with the details of the charges against Mr. Greenbelt?

Dorcas: In the matter of the People vs. Melvin Greenbelt, Mr. Greenbelt is accused of totally failing his parents, Miriam and Henry Greenbelt, in being a good son. I have a long list of serious charges, clear violations of the *Parent Protection Act.*

First, Melvin Greenbelt has failed to call his parents even once in the past 24 months. Second, Melvin doesn't answer their calls, even though they call daily—sometimes several times a day. Third, Mr. Greenbelt has totally neglected their birthdays and anniversaries. He hasn't sent them one penny, even though his mother tells me he is on the *Forbes Most Wealthy Americans* list. And now, Mr. and Mrs. Greenbelt are now living in a trailer next to a toxic waste dump.

Dee Fence: I object, your honor, that's all wrong. My client works in a shoe store!

Brighton: Objection sustained, continue

Dorcas.

Dorcas: Forth, the defendant has not let his parents visit their grandchildren, or taken his parents on any family vacations. And fifth, Melvin has been rude to his Aunt Bertha who has called him any number of times.

In summary your honor, and members of the Jury, Melvin Greenbelt is guilty of numerous egregious violations of the *Parent Protection Act*. The prosecution asks for a quick verdict of "guilty as charged."

Brighton: Dorcas, does the prosecution have witnesses they'd like to call?

Dorcas: Yes, your Honor. I would like to call the defendant's parents, Miriam and Henry Greenbelt. Can they take the stand together?

Brighton: I don't see why not. Bailiff, swear in the Greenbelts please.

After some shuffling to see who gets to sit closest to the judge, the Greenbelts are sworn in.

Dorcas: Now, Mr. and Mrs. Greenbelt, I'd like you to make a statement to the court. Remember, no fibbing or exaggerating, you are under oath.

Miriam: I'll talk first, your Attorneyship. You see, it's like this. Once upon a time we were a happy family. We did everything together. Through our hard work we paid for our son's education. It cost us our life savings and that's why we're so poor in our retirement, living in a drafty trailer and all. Then, after Melvin dropped out of medical school and got a high paying job, he began to systematically ignore us.

Dorcas: Can you be more specific?

Miriam: Do you think he would ever call? No. He specifically skips a nice dinner when I had invited Ruth Eisen just to meet him. He gave up practicing the piano despite all the money we spent on his lessons. We've not gotten a birthday card or a phone call for five years. He won't drive us to the doctor. And I won't even talk about my suggestion of having that tattoo removed!

Henry: He took our house and made us live in a trailer park, and our roof leaks and he won't have it fixed.

Miriam: And he won't let us babysit our grandchildren even though we offer. He won't attend synagogue on the holidays with us. His wife never calls and asks for a recipe.

Brighton: Okay, okay. I've heard enough. I'd like to hear what the defendant has to say for himself. Ms. Fence, will you please put your client, Melvin, on the stand. Bailiff, swear him in, please.

Melvin Greenbelt is sworn in

Dee Fence: Now Melvin. Tell the court what you think of these trumped-up charges.

Melvin: Lies and exaggeration, your Honor. I've been very kind to my parents although they don't deserve it sometimes. They drive me crazy, they always have. Ever since I was a little kid.

Dee Fence: Melvin, isn't it true you've been a good son and these charges are entirely false?

Melvin: Look, Judge, this whole thing is ridiculous. First of all, I was never in medical school, so how could I drop out? And I am not married, never have been, which I know is a source of aggravation to my parents. I have no kids and so there are no grandchildren to babysit. None! And as to dinners at their house, she is always trying to fix me up with some plain-Jane daughter of one her Mahjong club cronies. And every time I do come to dinner, I get sick eating her rich cooking. I'm a Vegan you know.

Dee Fence: Go on Melvin.

Melvin: And Your Honor, I've converted to Buddhism, and that's why I don't go to synagogue. I've never had a tattoo, and I took trumpet lessons, not piano. As to finances, I've been supporting them for years as best I can on my salary at the shoe store. You see, they sold their house, took the money and lost most of it at a casino on a senior citizen's bus trip to Atlantic City. I had to send them money to get home. Then I had to help them buy their trailer.

So I don't live in their house. It's not their house anymore. A couple named Racussen bought it. I went to school with their daughter.

Dee Fence: Melvin, that's enough. I think the jury can clearly see that you are innocent and that your parents ought to be ashamed bringing you to court like this.

Brighton: I've heard enough, too. Someone here is not telling the truth. It's time to turn the matter over to the Jury.

He explains the new law to the jury and gives them instructions before ordering them to the Jury room.

In the Jury room

It turns out that members of the Jury are a bunch of old farts and friends of Miriam and Henry

Greenbelt. They play Mahjong and Bridge together. and several Jury members belong to their Temple. So they kick around the evidence for a few minutes and then start playing cards, just so the judge won't think they are being too hasty. Lunch is brought in and several Jury members complain about the food.

Finally the card games are over and they signal that they are ready to come in and announce their verdict.

Brighton: Welcome back, members of the Jury. Will the Jury Foreman please rise and read the verdict.

Foreman: Yes, your honor. Based on the evidence and testimony, we have no choice but to find the defendant, Melvin Greenbelt, guilty as hell.

Melvin: What! This can't be.

Brighton: Will the defendant please rise? Mr. Greenbelt, Melvin, the Jury has found you guilty and you must pay the penalty under the law. I wish I could just sentence you to being a better son but I have to be more specific under the sentencing guidelines of the Parent Protection Act.

So, I hereby sentence you to a 20 minute phone call once per month. Also a four hour visit every three months. During that visit you will take them shopping.

Melvin: No...please, not that!

Brighton: Wait, I'm not done there's more. Melvin, you must drive them to the doctor when they ask you. Plus once every other year you will take them on a two week vacation to the resort of their choosing. Further, you will pay them $ 900 a month in parental support, make repairs to the roof of their trailer, and have their bathroom painted.

Melvin: No, no, Judge...that's unfair. I'm just a shoe salesman.

Brighton: Silence, Melvin! You will come to their Bridge club at the senior center and get shown off to their friends twice a year. And, you will drive them to synagogue and attend High Holiday services.

Melvin: Judge have a heart…

Brighton: Also, you will say "I'm sorry" for violating your parents' rights under the new law. All these punishments will run concurrently for the next seven years.

Brighton: What say you, Melvin?

Melvin: What can I say Judge? I'm not sorry. But I'll say it anyway. What choice do I have?

Brighton: Mr. and Mrs. Greenbelt, what say you?

Miriam: Yippee, your Honor. Come on Melvin, you have to take us to lunch and drive us back to the trailer park, so be a good boy. And thank you, Dorcas. And I thank the ASPCP* for bringing this case to court, and winning under the law they helped get passed. This will be a model for neglected parents everywhere.

Melvin: *(led away by his parents)* It's not a model, *(he shouts)* it's a diabolical law. The *Parent Protection Act* may be the most effective method of birth control ever invented!

*American Society for the Prevention of Cruelty to Parents.

A Christmas Tale

There is a Christmas song about Grandma – my Grandma, Ethyl. It's about how she got run over by one of Santa's reindeer. You might think it's made up but it really happened to Grandma. Seems she partied a little too much on Christmas Eve and left the house (without telling anyone) to get some much-needed fresh air. You'll never guess what happened next.

Claus: Ho, ho, ho. Holy crap, Dan. You're the lead reindeer. What the hell just happened here?

Dancer: I really didn't see her, Sandy. She was staggering across the lawn and I guess we ran over her when we landed.

Claus: Is she okay? Maybe we should call 911?

Dancer: I think she's going to be okay, Sandy. She's a bit dizzy and drunk as a skunk. Says her name is Ethyl Schwartz.

Claus: Ho, ho, ho, Ethyl. My name is Sandy. I

think you're going to be okay. Don't take this the wrong way, but I know that you've been drinking a bunch. In fact I know a lot about you.

Ethyl: You'd be drinking too if you had to spend Christmas Eve with a bunch of moron relatives! Say, who are you guys? Why are your reindeer pissing on my son's lawn? How do you know all about me? Why are you dressed so funny? What are you going to do about my coat and shoes your sled ruined when you ran me over?

Claus: Sorry about your coat, Ethyl. But at the North Pole we don't have a lot of cash. I can have my wife start a GoFundMe web campaign for a new coat if you like. Ethyl, I really regret that my sleigh and eight tiny reindeer, well, not so tiny, ran you over. How can my team and I make it up to you? I do grant wishes you know!

Ethyl: I'm getting a lawyer and suing your butt, Sandy. You have no business driving your sleigh on peoples' lawns and I don't care what day it is! Who is your insurance man, and do you have a license plate for that contraption?

Sandy: Now calm down, Ethyl. Don, do we have any water in the sleigh?

Donner: Let me check boss. Yes, here's a bottle of Ice Mountain Spring Water. Should still be cold.

Sandy: Here, Ethyl, take sip. Please.

Ethyl: Haven't you got anything stronger? I'll bet you've got a gift bottle of Cognac in your sleigh back there.

Sandy: We might. Vic, take a look, please.

Vixen: I found a bottle, boss. Here it is. Arnold Firsk is going to be disappointed.

Sandy: We'll leave him a Reindeer check, forgive the pun.

Ethyl: Tell you what, Sandy, (*takes a swig*) I'm not going back in that house. Take me with you wherever you're going and I'll forget that you mowed me down on the lawn like a garden gnome. I still want you to pay for my coat, though.

Sandy: Ethyl, you know what you're asking? This is Christmas Eve and we have deliveries to make all over the world.

Ethyl: Reindeer patties! No offense guys, but that bushwah is for kids. It's nearly ten o'clock and I doubt you'll get out of Oakland by midnight!

Sandy: You've got to believe, Ethyl. Right boys?

Reindeer: *Right, boss.*

Ethyl: Say, you haven't been shot at tonight, have you? This neighborhood is full of gun nuts looking for any excuse.

Sandy: No, Ethyl, not yet. Why don't you hop in next to me and we'll get on our way; maybe to a less violent neighborhood.

Ethyl: How are you getting down chimneys these days with the no-burn laws and gas fireplaces?

Sandy: We manage. Sometimes we use the back door, or an unlocked window; have to be quick. Especially if they have a dog; you should see the back of my pants.

Ethyl: Say, I know this house—don't stop here. Bunch of liberals live here.

Ethyl: And that house; snooty people, just give them lump of coal. Say, Sandy, what do you call a cat sitting on the beach on Christmas Eve? *Sandy Claws.*

Sandy: Oh, that's funny, Ethyl even the thousandth time I've heard it.

Ethyl: Well then. What do you call a bankrupt Santa?

Sandy: Let me guess: *Saint Nickel-less*. Right?
Ethyl: Sandy, your reindeers fart, did you know that? What else have you got to drink?

Sandy: Ethyl, can you please be quiet. I've got a lot of work to do and it's hard steering this old thing.

Ethyl: Do you know why aliens don't celebrate Christmas? *Because they don't want to give away their presence.* Ha!

Sandy: That's quite enough, Ethyl.

Ethyl: What kind of motorcycle does Santa ride? *A Holly Davidson.* Ha!
Sandy: Ethyl, I'm afraid we're going to have to take you back. You are a royal pain in the ass. And coming from Santa Claus who loves everybody, that is a rather harsh indictment.

C'mon team! Up Dasher, Dancer, Prancer, Vixen, Comet Cupid, Donner and…you, there, with the horns, in the front row.

Let's turn this ship around and dump, I mean take, Ethyl back to her son's house. I'll bet they're all really missing her.

Sandy knocks on the door. Ethyl is still singing and telling bad Christmas jokes. Her husband, George, answers the door.

George: Oh, you're back. For chrisakes, Ethyl. Do you have to get a snootfull at every party? Last month it was wild turkeys that attacked you in our back yard. Thank you, Sir, for bringing her home, I guess.

Sandy: Look, she's had a little accident. We'll send you a check for her coat and shoes.

George: Accident. Say, wait a minute. Who's fault was that? Can we get your name and address? Wait…

Sandy: (*running to the sled*) Merry Christmas to you all, and to all, a good night! C'mon guys, saddle up. We're outta here.

This is Phil's 5th book of humorous short stories. Phil is a retired management consultant. When he's not writing funny stories Phil, volunteers at the Local Community College and Performing arts Center. Phil and his wife, Alison, have lived in California's Sierra foothills for 17 years. It's much less crowded and expensive than the Bay Area where Phil grew up. And there are lots of wonderful writers and artists in the area. Meeting one or two them is one of Phil's goals for the coming year.

.

Made in the USA
San Bernardino, CA
24 February 2019